## Praise for I KNEW YOU'D BE LOVELY

"With humor, honesty, and wary hope, Alethea Black's stories capture the pain and power of loving fully—and celebrate life's small astonishments amid our shared human search for the divine. *I Knew You'd Be Lovely* is thoughtful, entertaining, and, ultimately, powerful."

—Daphne Kalotay, author of *Russian Winter*

"Alethea Black writes with a deceptively light touch, yet her work packs a serious punch . . . There's a spiritual hunger in her stories reminiscent of Flannery O'Connor, combined with a voice that is all her own."

—Sharon Pomerantz, author of *Rich Boy*

"Reading Alethea Black's seemingly effortless prose is like slipping into water—the eerily clear kind, that shows you more than you may want to see."

—Glen Hirshberg, winner of the 2008 Shirley Jackson Award

"Alethea Black can drop you into a dream with a single sentence, then convince you it's real. Her characters' best hopes and worst fears usually come to pass, often in fabulous ways, but their adventures feel inevitable and true—not only because Ms. Black richly imagines her people, but because she loves them. *I Knew You'd Be Lovely* is a lovely debut, with masterful prose and inspired invention on every page."

—Ralph Lombreglia, author of *Men Under Water*

"There's a touch of Lorrie Moore in Alethea Black's stories, but the voice is all her own. Black writes about love, yes, but she also writes about solitude—its travails and its pleasures—with a winning combination of insight and charm. *I Knew You'd Be Lovely* is a terrific debut."

—Joshua Henkin, author of *Matrimony*

# I Knew

## YOU'D BE

# Lovely

### STORIES

## Alethea Black

Broadway Paperbacks

NEW YORK

BROADWAY

Copyright © 2011 by Alethea Black

Published in the United States by Broadway Paperbacks,
an imprint of the Crown Publishing Group, a division of
Random House, Inc., New York.
www.crownpublishing.com

BROADWAY PAPERBACKS and its logo, a letter B bisected on the diagonal,
are trademarks of Random House, Inc.

Some of the stories in this book were originally published in
*American Literary Review, The Antioch Review, Arts & Letters,*
*The Chattahoochee Review, Green Mountains Review, Inkwell,*
*The Kenyon Review, Narrative, The North American Review,*
and *The Saint Ann's Review.*

Library of Congress Cataloging-in-Publication Data
Black, Alethea.
   I knew you'd be lovely : stories / Alethea Black.
      p.   cm.
   I. Title.
   PS3602.L243I3 2011
813'.6—dc22             2010033120

ISBN 978-0-307-88603-3
eISBN 978-0-307-88604-0

PRINTED IN THE UNITED STATES OF AMERICA

*Cover design by Erin Schell*

10   9   8   7   6   5   4   3   2   1

First Edition

*Dedicated in loving memory of David Palecek*

*to my sister Melissa and her four daughters:*

*Katrina, Caroline, Sierra, and Annika.*

# CONTENTS

At the still point of the turning world.

Neither flesh nor fleshless;

Neither from nor towards; at the still point,

there the dance is.

—T. S. Eliot

## THAT OF WHICH

## WE CANNOT SPEAK

Earlier that evening, under the pale streetlamps, Bradley had sat on a park bench and watched a row of trees carefully gathering snow. It was as if they were beckoning it, as though the snow were something they'd been wanting to say.

Now, speeding down Fifth Avenue in a cab whose driver seemed unaware of his own mortality, Bradley wished he were back on that park bench. Or in the diner they'd just passed. Or that police station. Anywhere but on his way to a party where strangers with cardboard hats and noisemakers always made him feel as if he were on the wrong planet.

It was 10:15 New York time, which meant it would already be 3:15 A.M. in Islington. Probably too late to call your ex-wife, even if she was most likely still out somewhere, sequined, laughing, ice making music in her glass. Besides, what would he say? "I'm sorry" was so easy and generic. Gail hated lack of specificity; in fact, this was one of the qualities that had drawn him to her in the first place. Whenever he used to overhear her on the phone with one of her sisters, she was always begging for details. "What were you wearing? What did he order? Did he leave a nice tip?"

Unfortunately, this need for particularity would later work against him. Toward the end, a therapist had pressed him to try to describe what was missing in their marriage. "It's ineffable," he'd said, at which point Gail stood up and shouted, "Well why don't you try effing it!" before she began to cry, softly, into her hands.

A professor once told him: "You must perpetually fight against the inexpressibility of it all," in a voice so solemn it gave Bradley a chill. But his deepest experiences always left him mute. Mute with appreciation, mute with anger, mute with awe. Consequently, even when he was in a wonderful relationship—a wonderful marriage, in fact—some part of him remained fundamentally alone. Once or twice, when there were still worlds of tenderness between them, he had lain awake after he and Gail made love, and while his wife slept beside him he shed silent, inexplicable tears. If Gail had awakened and discovered him, he wouldn't have known what to say.

As soon as he slammed the cab door, snowflakes began to speckle his head and coat. *One hour,* he said to himself, looking at his watch. His sole reason for coming to this party, given by a friend of a friend of a friend, was the affection and respect he held for Oscar. Oscar, whom he often thought of as irrational exuberance incarnate, also happened to be his financial advisor, and had stopped just short of bribery to enlist him. So against his better judgment he'd agreed to make an appearance.

On the eleventh floor, even before the elevator doors opened, he could hear the noise of the party. In the invitation, the music had been described, mystifyingly, as "post-funk sexycore yacht rock." At the end of a short hallway stood a tall blonde in a red sweater.

"Well, hello!" she said. "Do come in." Bradley knew that in spite of his bookish exterior he was, generally speaking, easy on the eyes. He followed her into the foyer. She was wearing black velvet pants, the tops of which were covered in bright red fuzz, as if her sweater were molting.

"You can put your coat in the back bedroom," she said close to his ear, in a party shout-whisper. She gestured, and for as far as the eye could see men and women bedecked in jewels and bow ties were sipping translucent drinks. They all looked to be in their mid- to late thirties. "I'm Evelyn, by the way," she said, extending her hand. "Kiki's sister."

"Bradley. Pleasure."

"Oh, you're English!" she said. Bradley smiled and excused himself. After placing his gift of Champagne on the only unoccupied countertop space, he deposited his overcoat in the bedroom, then began navigating his way back to the living room—*Excuse me, so sorry, beg your pardon.* In front of a large bay window overlooking the park stood a table blanketed with an array of foods. Each dish had a little calligraphied label: rosemary-rubbed chicken tenders, French ham and aged cheddar biscuits, duck-stuffed ravioli, truffle-kissed mini-pizzas. There was a gigantic chocolate torte in the center, which the host's uncle—he overheard an enthusiastic guest remark—had made by hand.

He pulled a china plate from the stack and would have begun to help himself but for the brunette standing in his way with her back to him. Not wishing to be rude, he waited for her to move, or turn sideways, or in some way reposition herself. Finally, he tapped her shoulder.

"Trying to decide what looks best?" he said. "It's all right if you sample them all. I won't tell."

The woman smiled and said nothing. Her eyes were smoky brown, and her hair was held back with two tortoiseshell combs. She continued to stand silently for a second before he noticed the clipboard hanging from her neck by a piece of brown packaging string.

*I can't speak,* it said at the top of a sheet of paper. *I have laryngitis.*

"Terribly sorry," he said. "I didn't realize."

The woman took up her clipboard and wrote with a pen tied to the end of the string: *No need to apologize.* Her handwriting was pretty, rounded and small. Bradley reached for the pen—*May I?* his raised eyebrows asked—and she let him have the clipboard. The fact that she was writing made him want to write. Monkey see, monkey do.

*Shouldn't you be home drinking tea with honey?* he scrawled, his left-handed cursive barely legible.

*Please, no more tea,* she wrote back. *No voice for 9 days. You realize how much tea that is?*

*9 days?* he wrote. *Perhaps you should see a doctor!* He handed her the pad.

*I am a doctor,* she said, and he blinked. She resumed writing. *What's your name?*

"Bradley," he said out loud, his voice awkward and unfamiliar to his own ear.

She nodded and turned away. She was wearing a strapless black dress and had a simple mother-of-pearl bracelet clasped about her writing wrist. But by far her most striking feature was her neck—long, bone white, flawless. Who knew what a throat like that might be capable of saying, if only it worked. She turned quickly and caught him staring at her. Taking the clipboard, she flipped to the final page, which was covered with prewritten words and phrases:

SAMANTHA
YES
NO
NOT SINCE 1979
KIKI AND I WENT TO GRADE SCHOOL TOGETHER
THAT'S WONDERFUL!
THAT'S HORRIBLE!
I KNOW JUST WHAT YOU MEAN
CAN'T SAY I EVER HAVE
HUMAN BEINGS ARE SO PREDICTABLE

She pointed to the first word.

"Well, hello there, Samantha," he said, offering his hand. He indicated the last entry, HUMAN BEINGS ARE SO PREDICTABLE, and gave her a quizzical look.

*We say the same things over and over,* she wrote.

*Love never repeats,* Bradley thought, but couldn't

remember where he'd read the phrase, and thought it best not to speak of love. "With so many words to choose from, you'd think we wouldn't perpetually use the same ones," he said in her ear, but with the noise of the party all around them, he couldn't tell if he was speaking inaudibly or assaulting her eardrum. Samantha apparently couldn't make out what he'd said; she moved closer to his mouth. Her head smelled powdery, like vanilla. Her ear was less than an inch from his lips; he could have kissed it if he'd wanted to. He repeated himself.

She nodded. *There used to be far fewer words, in primitive cultures. Past civilizations counted 1, 2, many.* She looked up at him. *Kind of how I calculate drinks,* she wrote.

"I assume you were a hieroglyphics major before you turned premed?" he said, wondering where the drinks were.

*Art history. Premed = after college (late bloomer). You?*

*Studied botany. Now botanist.*

As soon as she read this, Samantha stamped her foot, grabbed the pen, and began writing excitedly. She had a lot more enthusiasm than you'd think just from looking at her.

*You help me!* her clipboard proclaimed. *I furniture shopping, comparing diff. types wood. Salesman said pine = lots knots, oak = smoother grain, but couldn't say why.*

"Why?" Bradley said.

*Why,* she wrote again, and as he read the word, she leaned in to underline it. <u>*Why.*</u>

"Well, a pine branches in tiers, all the way up, whereas an oak sort of grows and then blooms at the top. A knot is where a branch meets the trunk," he said. "Like a shoulder," he added, touching two fingers to her collarbone.

Samantha's lips parted. *You have cast yourself as the bearer of wisdom,* she wrote, which made Bradley think: *If I'm the bearer of wisdom here, darling, we're both in a bucket of trouble.* "You might think less of me if you knew that earlier today it took all my wit and cunning to open a jar of pickles," he said, and her svelte torso jostled, but she made no sound.

Half an hour later, the air was hotter, the music louder, and the room more crowded. The party had become its own throbbing cocoon. Bradley and Samantha still stood in the center of the living room, passing the clipboard back and forth, only now they were also juggling colossal martinis. At one point a passerby had observed their antics and shouted: "Get a blackboard, you two!" Bradley was having a surprisingly good time. Sharing the clipboard with Samantha gave him a sense of stillness within the swirl of the party; it was like being in the eye of a storm, like being plugged in to the same iPod. Best of all, it made him feel as if the unspoken in him were connecting with the unspoken in her, and it crossed his mind that this was all chemistry ever was: two people's silent selves invisibly aligning while their noisy selves carried on, oblivious.

Samantha swallowed the last of her drink and wrote, *What made you leave the UK?*

"I came here about two years ago," he said. "Two years this past October."

*Not _when_. _Why?_*

"Oh, well, my personal circumstances changed," he said, and she looked at him as if he'd said he'd contracted a deadly disease. He finished his martini. *What the hell.* "My wife and I split," he said, and attempted to see if the playfulness had left her eyes. But Samantha was looking down, writing.

*Why?* Apparently a favorite question.

Bradley stared at the word. "Don't I at least get to refresh my drink before I answer that one?"

She nodded. *Go + get us a couple drinks, pls?*

On his way to the bar, he found himself imagining Samantha lying on his bed, her hair fanned out, her silence filling the air like humidity. While he waited to get the bartender's attention, he envisioned them having fantastic sex. "Kiss me when you're going to come," he would say, and later, she would—her long neck lifting in the kiss that said it all.

The music's bass notes were drumming through his very person. "I feel like my pancreas is vibrating!" he shouted in the direction of the bartender, trying to be friendly. But the compact man just stared at him as if he were an affront to the world's efficiency. "Two," Bradley mouthed, holding up his fingers in a *V.*

"How'd you lose your voice?" he said, handing Samantha her third martini.

*Marlboro reds. 2 packs/day.*

"That's an interesting habit for a physician."

She grinned. *Kidding!* she wrote. *I'm pulmonary specialist. Tell patients smoking = suicide for procrastinators. Had flu 2 days then woke up—no voice. Now tell why you + wife split.*

"You don't give up easily, do you?" he said. He realized he was already a good bit drunk. "My ex-wife claims I'm no good at sharing my inner life."

Samantha's face still gave the faint impression of a smile, even though she was no longer smiling.

*Is she right?*

"I suppose she is," he said. During one of their quieter fights, Gail had accused him of having the communication skills of an elm. "You can't always expect people to read your mind," she said. "It isn't fair."

*Makes for a lonely life,* Samantha wrote.

"It's a fruitless task, explaining yourself," he said. He was enjoying confessing the truth for once. "Either people get you, or they don't. In fact, even when they get you, it's always . . ." *Partial,* he wanted to say. *Imperfect. A disappointment.*

*You may never be 100% understood. I'd settle for 55%. But you shouldn't be afraid to speak your heart. Not to a woman you love.*

She gave him a serious look, and he sensed a clinical aspect to her. His floaty, liberated feeling was being undermined by a light panic, as though something old in him were dueling with something new. He noticed she'd begun glancing around as if she were expecting someone. Or searching for an opportunity to escape. He was losing her.

In a large room off to the left, the hosts had hung a

seventies-style disco ball. The DJ was still spinning, and Bradley was weighing the merits of inviting Samantha to dance when a sweaty man in a cummerbund came jogging backward and barreled into him. Bradley stumbled and spilled his entire drink down the front of Samantha's dress. Her throat made a croaky, voiceless gasp.

"Oh, God! I'm so sorry. Let me get you a washcloth. Hold on, I'll be right back," he said. Samantha had begun to write a reply, but he didn't stay to read it.

When Bradley returned from the kitchen with a hand towel and a bottle of seltzer, Samantha was gone. His pulse quickened. He scanned the room, but she was nowhere.

Wait a minute—there she was, over in the corner. Someone else was already attending to her—two men, in fact—and she was touching their arms, and laughing, and stamping her foot, just as she had with him. Of course. Why not? Hadn't it only been in his head, the sense of unique connection? What made him assume she shared it? It was clear to him now that her curious enthusiasm existed quite independently of him. It was simply who she was.

Perhaps because of the cold, the other partygoers were neglecting the terrace, a slender consolation. He closed the sliding glass door and stood alone under the falling snow. Without calculating the time in Islington, he took out his mobile.

She picked up on the fifth ring. "Gail, hi, it's me, it's Bradley," he said. He was speaking quickly, trying not to overthink. He was desperate to recapture the liberated feeling. "Listen, I . . ." What meaningful thing could he possibly say to her now? He stared through the condensation-coated glass at the revelers. He knew they were only a few meters away, but it felt as if the distance between him and them were greater than the distance to the moon.

"I'm sorry I couldn't give you what you wanted," he said.

Gail didn't yell at him for waking her up. She didn't say: "Oh, God, Bradley," or "Are you drunk?" She wasn't dramatic like that; it wasn't her style. That was one of the things he'd loved best about her.

"What is it you think I wanted, Bee?" she said. She hadn't used his nickname in a long while; it hurt to hear it. Bradley closed his eyes. Of all the people in the world, Gail had probably understood him best.

"I wanted *you,* that's all," she said.

He could barely keep his thoughts straight, but he knew it had all gone wrong somehow. "I don't know what to do," he said.

"I don't understand what you mean."

"I feel lost in this world," he whispered.

Gail was silent for a moment. "It isn't altogether impossible, you know."

"What isn't?"

"To trust people." Her voice sounded surprisingly calm, even beautiful. For one wild instant, he thought about asking: *Is it too late for us?* But he knew it was.

He was nodding in the half-light, but of course Gail couldn't see him. He thought he heard a man's voice in the background, and her muffled reply: "It's Bradley." His breath came out in small white bursts. There was one more thing.

"Are you happy?" he said.

There was a pause. "Yes," she said, and he knew it was the truth. He felt both pained and relieved.

"I'm glad," he said. "You deserve it."

"Bradley!" a voice bellowed from the direction of the food. It was Oscar, with a blonde under one arm and a redhead under the other. He kissed Bradley on both cheeks. "I can't believe you showed up! You are my favorite person in the whole world!" He seemed even more drunk than Bradley, which was saying something. "Are you just getting here?" he said, and Bradley knew he would have to find a way to break it to him that he was wearing his coat because he was on his way out. "Why in God's name don't you have a drink? Here."

"What's this?"

"Ouzo and Sprite," Oscar said. "Drink it." He began introducing the girls. "These are Cricket"—he put his hand on the back of the blonde—"and Jackie." He patted the redhead.

"Hiya," said Jackie.

"Hello," said Cricket.

Oscar released them, pulled an arm around Bradley's shoulders, and nodded in the direction of a pregnant woman. "Have I ever told you I think women are like flowers and pregnant women are like fruit?"

Jackie whacked him on the arm with the backside of her hand.

"What?" he said. "What's wrong with that? There's nothing offensive about that!"

"There most certainly is," Jackie said.

"Hey, you're Laryngitis Girl!" Cricket said, spotting the clipboard. A second later, Samantha had joined the group. "I heard someone talking about you when I first came in, but I thought they made it up. I thought you were a party myth!"

Samantha slowly shook her head. *Nope, I'm real,* she seemed to be saying.

Oscar extended his hand. "I am Oscar, lovely lady. And this fine fellow is my dear friend Bradley—"

"We've met," Bradley said. "We were talking for a while. Before." Samantha handed him her clipboard.

*Were you planning on leaving without saying good-bye?*

"Of course not. I was about to go looking for you," he said. From her face he could tell she knew he was lying. He took a sip of the ouzo and Sprite; it tasted dreadful.

Jackie was observing them. "Hey, wouldn't it be funny if you two became fast friends, only then her voice came back, and you couldn't stand the sound of it?" she said, apparently very excited by the idea. Bradley and Samantha stood motionless. Oscar pressed his lips together.

"I don't mean timelessly funny," she said. "Just, you know, funny in a Seinfeldian sort of way."

"Wasn't there a princess in some fairy tale who had to give up her voice to save the thing she loved?" Cricket said.

"Like what—a prince?" said Jackie. Oscar laughed, and Cricket shrugged. Samantha began to write.

*Who were you talking to out there?*

"My wife," Bradley said. "I mean, my ex-wife." God.

"Listen, things are over between my wife and me. They have been for a long time."

*You don't have to explain yourself to me,* Samantha wrote, but he noticed she wouldn't meet his gaze.

Cricket craned her neck to see the clipboard. "Can I buy a vowel? Can I buy a vowel?" she said, and Bradley's head began to throb. Had he eaten anything today, other than pickles?

Jackie snapped her fingers. "Listen up," she said, addressing the group. "See if you can come up with the word that makes use of all the vowels—in their proper order."

Oscar took off his glasses and began cleaning them with his handkerchief.

"Including *Y*?" Cricket asked.

"Including *Y*," Jackie said, taking a hearty gulp from her drink.

Bradley handed the ouzo and Sprite back to Oscar. It now felt as if tiny elves were constructing an aquarium inside his skull. "Have you by chance got any aspirin?" he asked Samantha, trying to summon a smile.

*Sorry. Guess I'm not much of a doctor.* She looked him in the eye for the first time. *You OK?*

"I've got a bit of a headache," he said, wishing he could tell her everything—that she was the first woman he'd been attracted to since his wife, that the reason he'd moved to the States was so he could officially become a foreigner, since he'd felt like one his whole life.

"Give us a clue," Oscar said to Jackie. He loved riddles and did the *Times* crossword religiously.

"There are no clues," Jackie said. Cricket made a frown with puckered lips. "Okay, fine. It begins with the letter *F*. And that's just because I like you guys."

"*Faeoli*," Oscar said.

"Not a word!" said Jackie. "And don't try to get funny with me."

Oscar turned to Bradley. "You all right there, buddy? You're not looking so hot."

"I'll be all right," Bradley said, but then felt his stomach fluids reverse direction, as if in a gastrointestinal Coriolis effect.

"*Facetiously,*" Jackie announced, and Oscar cursed. Bradley scanned the room to see where a bathroom might be.

"Hey, it's almost midnight!" Cricket said. Instinctively Bradley turned toward Samantha. She was gone again.

"Where'd she go?" he said, grabbing Oscar by the shoulders. "That girl who was just here."

"I saw her putting her coat on in a hurry. I think her pager went off or something."

So he'd lost her for real this time. The room began to spin. "I've got a terrific headache," he said.

"Wow," Cricket said. "Did you know those were FDR's last words?"

Not at all relieved by this information, Bradley felt as if he were about to vomit. "Where's the bathroom?" he asked, concentrating on the floor.

"Over by the kitchen, where you first came in," said Jackie.

When he got there, he found a heartbreaking queue. "Ten, nine, eight," the crowd began to chant. Bradley pushed his way to the front, hoping they'd be too festive to notice. "Seven, six, five." *This is a medical emergency,* he was prepared to offer, if anyone objected. "Four, three, two." He saw the door open, shoved past the person who was leaving—"One"—and barely had time to turn the lock before dropping to his knees. "Happy New Year!" the crowd cheered, as Bradley retched.

He lay on the floor for what seemed like a long time, blurry and exhausted, his thoughts weaving everywhere. *Can I buy a vowel? Can I buy a vowel?* On the other side of the door, the sound of popping corks punctuated the flow of songs and laughter. He was spending the first moments of a newborn year in the fetal position on the floor of a stranger's bathroom. He breathed in the cold, lonely smell of tile and tried to imagine what he might have said or done differently. He remembered something he'd been taught as a child: that in the end, we'll be judged by our dreams as well as our accomplishments, by all that went unspoken as well as what was said. But even as a Catholic schoolboy, he'd rejected the idea as both sentimental and unlikely. And now, with an acrid taste still fresh in his mouth, he rejected it anew. Sometimes things simply didn't work out. Wasn't that just the way of the world? Sometimes you try and try until your heart might break, and still your shot at heaven slips away.

Someone was pounding on the door. Bradley didn't care. He remained on the floor, staring at a loofah sponge and some pink bath-oil beads that must have belonged to Kiki.

"What's going on in there?" a man's voice shouted, and then swiftly, silently, a piece of paper slid under the door.

*I have something for you.*

Bradley rose and undid the lock, and there, at the front of the crowd, stood Samantha, with her coat still on. She held out her hand and smiled. In it was a bottle of aspirin.

He wanted to speak but couldn't. *How does one begin?* he wanted to ask her. *How does anyone ever begin?* Samantha's body seemed to answer for her: She took his hand and led him down the hallway, into the elevator, and out the front door.

After the crowded noise of the party, the stillness of the street came as a shock. The snow had stopped falling, and everything—from the trash receptacles to the parked cars to the streetlamps—had been transformed into a fresh version of itself. It was beautiful; it was like waking up into a snowman's dream of Earth.

Samantha slipped her arm through his, and the two began to walk. "Where to?" he said. She leaned in and gave him a quick peck on the cheek. So the pair continued, arm in arm, with no clue where they were going, and no idea what they were in for. But in a way, it didn't seem to matter, and for many city blocks, neither one of them said a word.

# THE ONLY WAY OUT

# IS THROUGH

The camping trip was Fetterman's idea. Carla had reached the end of her rope months ago and had been looking into one of those hard-core rebellious-teen boot camps, where the unspoken motto seemed to be that you have to be broken before you can be fixed. But then there was a death at the very camp they'd researched: A boy named Martin Lee Anderson—who was also fifteen and even looked a little like Derek—had died after collapsing during a march and then being kicked in the abdomen by one of the counselors. There was a lawsuit, and a *20/20* exposé, and it quickly became clear to both Fetterman and Carla that perhaps tough love was not the answer.

Out of desperation, and maybe a little out of self-loathing, Fetterman decided to confide his child-rearing woes to his ex-wife, a psychoanalyst still living and practicing in their old colonial in Wellesley, Massachusetts. It needled him to think of her in that house. They'd bought it as a fixer-upper, then spent the next seven years accosted by constant noise, clutter, and inconvenience. And dust—at one point they discovered sawdust even in the empty ice-cube trays in the freezer. By the time the renovations were complete, the marriage had fallen apart. Sonya offered to split the house—let him have the upstairs and she'd keep the downstairs, and her practice—but this seemed the sort of arrangement that kept psychoanalysts in business, and Fetterman didn't bite. Instead he packed his bags and moved to Arizona.

Sonya was a highly respected therapist who'd first become interested in the field when her college roommate told her she gave exquisite advice. She had a way of making her patients feel she was always on their side, deep down, even if she disagreed with them on the surface. Which had made it all the more objectionable to Fetterman that it felt as if she were secretly against him, waiting for him to screw up—and now he finally had, as predicted. Telling her that things had gone from bad to unbearable with Derek, that they'd lost control of him, that they'd even considered one of those boot camps, was as close to self-flagellation as he had ever come. No wonder he could only bear to do it via e-mail. His ex-wife meted out her disapproval succinctly: "When you correct others don't humiliate them. Show them new tenderness; then they will humble themselves." At first Fetterman had dismissed such lofty naïveté—and from a woman with no children of her own—but in short order began to accuse himself of a possible failure of imagination. A few days later, racking his brain for ways to try "new tenderness," he'd conceived of the camping trip.

Fetterman worked in tech support and had never been

on a camping trip, but it seemed the sort of excursion on which a father and son might reconnect. In his old life, he might even have imagined a touching lesson imparted while fishing, or a tender explanation of the constellations in the night sky, or a reconciliation after a near-death experience—perhaps a bear attack, or an unsuccessful river fording. In his old life, that is, before he'd had to apologize to the neighbor whose cat Derek lit on fire, before he'd had to explain to a third-grade teacher that there was no way his son had access to actual anthrax. Before his understanding of the world and its inhabitants had been completely transformed.

Fetterman saw no reason to let a simple lack of experience stand in his way. On his lunch hour he drove to the bookstore in the strip mall down the road from his office and picked up *Wilderness Camping & Hiking: The Ultimate Outdoors Book.* The store was out of *Camping for Dummies,* which was fine by Fetterman; one of his overachiever classmates had patented the franchise, and Fetterman would sooner have been bastinadoed (*Medieval Torture for Dummies*) than add to that guy's profit stream.

He sat on a footstool and flipped through the pages, stopping at a diagram that showed how to use your jeans as a backpack by roping the waist and bringing the legs up over your shoulders as straps. The chapter featured all kinds of ingenious solutions to unlikely scenarios; "In Case of Emergency," it was called. Fetterman closed the book, thinking: *Isn't life just one big, long emergency, happening very, very slowly?* He bought a carrot muffin and an iced coffee and browsed the rest of the store, skipping the comic book section, of course. The only other book he considered buying was a memoir showcased among the new releases. It was written in the form of a letter from a mother to her runaway teenage daughter. On the back, a savvy blurb read: "Every fifteen-year-old is a runaway, whether she runs away or not." Fetterman returned the volume to the shelf. Best not to give the boy any new ideas.

Fetterman and Derek had been in the car for an hour and a half. Derek had yet to speak. He sat in the backseat, surly in his headphones, practically a caricature of teen angst. If Fetterman hadn't put away his pencils for good, he might have been inspired to try to capture the embattled disinterest on his son's features. He stole furtive glances in the rearview mirror: Derek had no nose piercings, no Mohawk, no black eyeliner, no trench coat. His face was so nakedly defiant, it was as if he didn't need the props.

It was not an unattractive face. As an infant, Derek had been the most beautiful baby. Everyone remarked on it. And so placid; he seemed to possess an otherworldly calm. "That boy is a Rembrandt cherub!" said a barista with horn-rimmed glasses the first Saturday Fetterman and Carla took him out into the world. That Derek had been such a well-behaved, delightful baby was one of the most painful ironies of their current situation. Carla had once gazed into his eyes the way a woman who has lived her whole life in the mountains would gaze at the sea. Now she'd started taking five milligrams of Valium every morning, and still it didn't stop her hands from shaking.

"Jesus!" said Fetterman, swerving just in time. A deer was standing in the middle of the road. In the backseat, Derek remained unfazed. They rounded a curve and passed a deer warning sign. "Little late now," Fetterman muttered. He'd always thought deer warning signs had a lot more artistry than other road signs; the deer were rendered in much greater detail than humans. Derek took off his headphones, and Fetterman seized the opportunity to ask him a question. "Do you know why deer graze so close to the road?" he said, regretting that his earnest attempt at conversation sounded like the setup to a joke. Derek ignored him, made a minute technical adjustment, and put the headphones back on. Fetterman answered anyway. "Because the grass is saltiest there, especially in winter," he said, a fact he'd learned in his defensive driving course. "It's the foie gras of grass." He could hear the metallic screed of what sounded like a symphony of Bessemer converters. There were still two hours to go before they reached Lockett Meadow, and he suspected they would spend it in silence.

By the time they passed the first sign for Flagstaff, Fetterman was already wondering if the trip was a mistake. He hated outdoor activities and tried to avoid them as much as possible. Once, when he and Sonya were first courting, she'd invited him on a ski getaway with two other couples. Fetterman had pointed out that skiing combined three things he loathed—extreme cold, extreme height, and extreme speed—but agreed to go anyway. He spent the majority of the weekend in a foul mood, watching stand-up comics on HBO while Sonya and her friends donned Thinsulate and tested the strength of their anterior cruciate ligaments. He figured he had only himself to blame: He should have said no. Bad things happened when you followed the crowd. Maybe he would say that to Derek at some point over the weekend, tell him that he agreed in principle with wanting to strike out on your own, rebel against everything, find your drummer, but it was possible to do so in a less destructive way. In his head, he searched for phrases that wouldn't sound pedantic and square. Then he tried to imagine what would have happened if his own father had ever said such a thing to him.

Fetterman had been a wayward teenager himself—*Who wasn't?* he liked to ask, when telling stories of his youth—and had never really connected with his father, who worked in radio and died shortly after Fetterman went to college. In fact, the closest he'd felt to him was an experience that took place when his father was absent. It happened on an afternoon in the summer of 1977, when Fetterman was seventeen. He'd just had a blowout fight with his girlfriend and had gone for a long walk on the jetty in Gloucester, Massachusetts. He thought he was alone, but then he spotted an old man fishing by himself at the end of the pier. The old-timer had a radio with him, and when Fetterman approached, he looked up at him with watery blue eyes. "Elvis is dead," he said. Fetterman's first instinct was to run home and tell his father the news. His father had worshipped Elvis, had gotten his first job in radio in the 1950s after seeing Elvis on *The Ed Sullivan Show.* But by the time he got home,

Fetterman realized, his father would already know. If he didn't know now. He looked at the old man sitting alone, and suddenly he understood: His father *did* know; he could feel it. "Elvis is dead, Pop," he said, staring across the wide, churning surface of the ocean. His father died of a heart attack the following year.

Fetterman needed to use the bathroom and fill the gas tank. He got off at a rest area in McGuireville, stepping out of the car with one hand at his lower back. The rush of heat took him by surprise. Twenty years in the desert, and most days he still felt like a Yankee. He opened Derek's door and a strange smell spilled from the car that he hadn't noticed while in it.

"Time to do your business," he said, not hearing until the words had left his mouth that this was language usually reserved for dogs. Derek continued to stare angrily at nothing. "I'm going to use the men's room," Fetterman said, hooking his thumbs in his belt loops. "This may be our last chance for a while. Care to take advantage?" Derek yanked the door shut.

Outside the men's room there was a warning sign about poisonous snakes and insects; the drawing pictured a coiled rattler and a scorpion. An oddly placed reminder that there was no escaping danger, even during the most banal activities. When he was reading up on campgrounds, Fetterman had learned how to deal with an aggressive mountain lion—wave your arms, throw rocks, but *never run*—and that kangaroo rats were so efficient at recycling the fluid in their bodies that they sometimes urinated crystals. What exactly was a kangaroo rat? He wasn't sure he wanted to know. The tone of some of the writing had surprised him. In addition to the vermilion cliffs and house-sized boulders described at Toroweap, it also said that the Colorado River was only thirty seconds away—"a 30-second, 1,200-foot free fall, that is!" Ah, the old gleefully-awaiting-the-Apocalypse approach. Fetterman marveled that he had once found this attitude amusing.

When he returned to the car, the door handle lifted flimsily; the door remained shut. Derek had locked him out. "Unlock the car, Derek," he said, sighing heavily, regretting that he'd left the keys in the ignition in case his son needed some air. Without making eye contact, Derek gave him the finger. You'd think they'd beaten him as a child, or made him shovel feces in a hundred-degree factory from dawn to midnight. Instead he'd had the most comfortable middle-class upbringing imaginable. Where did it come from, the sea of rage within? "I'm serious," Fetterman said, pulling repeatedly on the impotent handle. "We need to get going so we can make it before dark." As it was, it was unclear how much time he'd need to pitch the tent and set up camp. Fetterman had been ready to leave at two, but Carla, a physician's assistant, had insisted on putting together a homemade first-aid kit, and spent twenty minutes showing him how to make a proper tourniquet.

Aside from giving him the finger, Derek was unresponsive. Fetterman gathered his thoughts and tried to keep a lid on his frustration. He knew from tech support that solutions always presented themselves sooner or later; the trick was not to lose your head. Instead of supplying Derek with whatever reaction the child was trying to provoke, he'd just wait him out. He sat down on the pavement, not a good idea—that must be what fiery brimstone felt like—and immediately stood up. It was so hot the soles of his sneakers were tacky against the asphalt. "Open the door!" he yelled, just as a mother heaved herself out of a Buick station wagon that had pulled in beside him. She had a gaggle of kids in the back; there must have been five or six, all under the age of sixteen.

"He lock you out?" the woman said. Fetterman nodded, and her face curled as if the act of defiance had been performed by one of her own brood. "I tell you, what that child needs is a good whupping. Open the door, you little shit!" she said, slapping the window. Her kids gathered around the car with their bruised shins and neon flip-flops. "Open the car, you little shit!" one of the girls shouted. She kicked a tire while one of the older boys hit Derek's window again. Then a different boy slapped the rear bumper, and before Fetterman knew what was happening, they'd all joined in, chanting: "Open the car! Open the car! Open the car!" while they rocked the vehicle and pounded on the glass.

"That's enough!" Fetterman shouted. All of them stopped at once. "This is between us. I'll take care of it." The mother sniffed, and the pack headed for the 7-Eleven, but their energy didn't change, it only shifted, and they walked away pinching and pushing one another.

You'd think there would have been some gratitude for the rescue, but if anything, Derek became more intractable than ever, and still wouldn't unlock the door. Fetterman removed his cell phone from a holster attached to his belt.

"Derek, I'm going to call Triple-A now, and I'm going to tell them that I'm locked out of my car. They will tell me they'll be here within half an hour, and then they will come, and unlock the door, and you will have to sit there while they do." Derek didn't seem to care. Fetterman dialed and made the report. Two minutes after he hung up, Derek rolled down the window and hurled the keys at the pavement. Fetterman called Triple-A back and told them their services were no longer needed. Then he picked up the keys and got in the driver's seat. He spun around to face Derek.

"Talk to me," he said, putting his hand on the boy's knee.

"Just leave me alone!" Derek was close to tears. "All I fucking want is to be left alone!"

Fetterman started the car, wondering why Derek had agreed to come in the first place. "I can't leave you alone," he said. "I'm your father. I have to deal with you, whether I like it or not."

Once they were back on the road, the troubleshooting part of Fetterman's brain tried to come up with ways to solve the communication problem. It was true, they didn't talk; Derek never told him anything about his life. All Fetterman knew was that some of his friends looked like hoodlums in training. Derek had been in therapy since he was six, without much success. Fetterman wasn't surprised; he didn't think much of the entire enterprise. He'd once shown his first wife a cartoon he drew, called "Jesus in Therapy." The psychoanalyst was asking: *What about* you, *what about* your *needs? Are you going to keep letting people walk all over you like this?* Sonya had frowned and accused him of being passive-aggressive.

Of course, Fetterman didn't tell his son much about his own life, either, but it seemed the boy didn't *want* to know him. One morning at breakfast he'd broken the silence to say: "I used to be in a band." But then the silence had descended again, and Fetterman felt pathetic—the epitome of pathetic, pathetic's apogee. In fact, Pathetic's Apogee would have been a better name for their band, instead of Hair of the Dog. *We weren't that bad,* he wanted to tell his son, and they weren't. They'd even booked a bunch of gigs, and had a small following. In 1993 Fetterman had played the drums in half the clubs in Arizona.

When Fetterman turned west off SR 89, Lockett Meadow was only twenty minutes away. He passed a slow-moving Subaru with a bumper sticker that read: I'M ALREADY AGAINST THE NEXT WAR. Then he passed a pair of hitchhikers. Fetterman had hitchhiked once, after something he said had so pissed off Carla that she took the car and left him at the Lone Coyote. Fetterman had no money in his wallet because he'd already spent it buying her milk-and-Kahlúa cocktails all night. In many ways, Carla and Sonya were perfect opposites. Where Sonya was hyperintellectual, Carla read *In Touch* magazine. While Sonya had cycled through being macrobiotic and vegan and militantly organic, Carla ate McDonald's hamburgers. Even physically, they were reverse: Sonya with her black helmet of hair and sharp nose, Carla with her frosted bangs and Cupid's-bow mouth. Fetterman had thought marriage to Carla would be easy after all the mind games with Sonya, but all marriages are difficult at times, just in different ways. The most important difference between his wives was that Carla wasn't one for grudges. And she didn't fault him for not living up to some imaginary potential.

He wasn't a complete failure as an artist. He'd had one breakthrough: *The New Yorker* had plucked one of his cartoons from the slush pile. It featured a well-dressed couple sipping cocktails at a fancy restaurant. The man's caption read: *On the contrary, most men's lives of desperation are not nearly quiet enough.* But Fetterman had never been able to make a living at it, and when he had to reenter the dating pool after his marriage broke up, he decided to get a real job and quit cartooning for good. Not because Sonya had screamed: "Everything's a joke to you, even our marriage!" the day she told him she was filing for divorce, but because there comes a stage in life when you have to be more realistic. Not everyone makes it. Or, as his magazine editor friend liked to say: Many answer; few are called.

When they arrived at the campsite, Derek refused to get out of the car. Fine. Fetterman would set up the tent, and Derek could join him if he wanted. If not, he could bivouac in the Nissan. He fished the instructions out of the trunk. Step 1: Find a flat, dry area. Well, at least Step 1 sounded reasonable. He set out in search of a suitable spot, this time taking the car keys with him, after rolling down the windows. In the distance, the San Francisco Peaks loomed like a huge set of problems they hadn't even gotten to yet. There was the temptation to give up, to say, "We tried our best," and be done with it. Perhaps it was just as noble simply to let things play themselves out, one way or another. His own father, who mostly interacted with Fetterman through his mother, would never have indulged such disobedience. Rarely a presence at his games, his dad happened to be sitting at the kitchen table the day Fetterman came home with his first Little League uniform. His dad eyed the shirt. "Eighty-eight means hugs and kisses in ham radio," he said. Fetterman didn't know what to do with this information; it vaguely made him want to trade numbers, but it was too late for that. The comment—not the meaning, but the intent—baffled him then, as it baffled him now. His father must have said other things to him over the course of their eighteen years together, but on some days, "Eighty-eight means hugs and kisses" was all he could remember.

He found the perfect spot, about five hundred feet from the car. Not bumpy, not wet, but dry and flat, with a tree nearby. A Goldilocks spot. He headed back to get the tent, but when he was still several yards away, he stopped. He knew something was wrong even before his mind could register what it was. Then he saw: Derek was holding a gun. The barrel was pointed at his own temple.

"Derek," he said. To his horror, he observed that the boy's hand was not shaking. It was Fetterman's hands that had begun to tremble. "Don't do this," he said.

"This way you won't have to deal with me anymore," said Derek.

"You know I didn't mean that the way it sounded," Fetterman said. Derek wouldn't look at him. "Son, whatever it is, we can get through it. I'll try harder, things will be different—"

"Save it!" Derek shouted. "I already know all the bullshit, and I can tell you, I'm not interested. There isn't one fucking word that could come out of your mouth that would possibly interest me." It occurred to Fetterman that his son must have been preparing for this—perhaps for a long time. He felt his body go blank. Derek's eyes squeezed shut.

"We didn't want you," Fetterman said. "You were unplanned. We had only been married a month when your mom found out she was pregnant. Things were just getting going with my job, and—" He paused. "We didn't think we were ready for a child. We wanted more time." He let out a laughlike huff. "And then you came early. I was playing a gig in Tucson when your mother called to say she was going into labor." Derek was still holding the gun. His eyes were still closed. But he was listening. "You were born on July fifth, but it was after midnight—really, it was the night of July fourth. I left the club and made it from Tucson to Phoenix in just over an hour. For the entire drive, the sky was exploding. There were fireworks going off on both sides of the road, for miles and miles. And they weren't ordinary fireworks, they were"—Fetterman felt his throat constrict—"beautiful," he said. "It was the most beautiful sky I've ever seen." Now that the words were out, his face collapsed. "Please don't do this. I'm begging you. Not as a father to a son. As a brother to a brother."

"You didn't want me," Derek said. "That's perfect, that's fucking priceless."

"Not at first," Fetterman said. "But when you arrived, it was the best thing that ever happened to us. Sometimes you don't know what you want until you get it." He swallowed. "I know you're in pain," he said.

"You don't know anything!"

"Then tell me. Tell me how I can help you." Derek made no motion and no sound; it was possible he was considering. "Tell me what to do," Fetterman said, slowly moving closer to the car.

"I just want to be left alone!" Derek said. His arm slackened a little. Fetterman continued his advance.

"We can make it better. But not if you end it. If you end it now, it will never get any better than this."

As Fetterman reached the car, Derek broke down. Fetterman opened the door. "Give me the gun," he said. Derek was crying silently, his chest heaving. He handed the gun to his father and continued to sob. Fetterman locked the weapon in the glove compartment and sat in the car with his son.

"Do you want to talk?" he said.

"I want to go home."


On the way back to Phoenix, Fetterman stayed fifteen miles below the speed limit. His body ached as if he'd just run a marathon; he drove like an old man. He *was* an old man. A gun. Where on Earth had Derek gotten such a thing? He'd save the interrogation for the morning; tonight he was too exhausted, and he still had the three-hour drive ahead of him. His ambition was singular: Bring the child safely home. Still, the feel of the weapon's heft lingered in his hand. One of Carla's friends, an army medic, had recently shipped off to Iraq, and before she left, her commanding sergeant told her to take as many Tampax as she could fit in her suitcase. Apparently they were perfect for plugging bullet wounds in the field and stanching the flow of blood.

In the rearview mirror, he caught Derek surreptitiously flipping through the camping book. He was probably reading about the poisonous mushrooms with names like angel destroyer and jack-o'-lantern, or how snakes have been known to inflict fatal bites by reflex action even after death. Fetterman and Carla agreed: Their son had a bizarre attraction to the medically macabre. When Derek was in the sixth grade, Fetterman had to have an appendectomy. His son came running after him before he left for the hospital; Fetterman thought it was to say good-bye. "Dad, did you know that you can wake up while they're operating on you, and feel the pain of everything, but not be able to talk?" Fetterman did not know this; in fact, he hoped it wasn't true. Derek went on about how redheads were more resistant to anesthesia than other people, and how the inventor of anesthesia had gotten the idea from Genesis, the part where it said that God put Adam into a deep sleep before removing his rib.

By that point, Fetterman and Carla already knew that their son was going to give them trouble. What they didn't know, what they had no way of knowing, was that the rebellion and the acute pain of adolescence would pass, but that the fascination with medicine would endure; that their son would go on to become a doctor, who in the course of his lifetime would help bring thousands of people out of their suffering. On the way to the hospital, Fetterman had turned to his wife. "Is that true, about the anesthesia wearing off?" he said. "It's extremely rare," Carla said.

As they drew close to home, on the narrow stretch of 117, at almost the exact spot where they'd passed the deer before, they came upon a dead deer in the road. Fetterman pulled over and put on his hazards. He got out of the car and grabbed the animal by its legs, but he was weak, and the deer was heavier than he'd expected. "Help me," he said to Derek. Derek took the front legs and Fetterman took the rear, and together they began to drag the deer to the shoulder. Halfway there, Derek stopped.

"She's still alive," he said.

"That doesn't matter!" Fetterman snapped. It was dangerous to be standing in the middle of the road, in the dark, just ahead of a curve. "Help me get her across."

From the safety of the side of the road, Fetterman could see that his son was right: The limbs were supple and freighted with life; the eyes still had light in them. But the body was broken. In the distance, he could hear coyotes' yips and yowls. Derek was waiting for him to speak.

"Get the gun," Fetterman said, handing him the keys. Derek obeyed, and a moment later, Fetterman was holding the weapon. Derek knelt beside the wounded animal, staring into its face as if he recognized something. Then he stood back. Fetterman had never fired a gun before. He placed the muzzle between the doe's brown eyes, braced himself, and pulled the trigger.

# GOOD IN A CRISIS

At night, for an hour before going to sleep, Ginny read the personal ads. Not because she was looking for a lover, but because she was mesmerized by the language people chose to describe themselves. She found herself underlining standout lines by women and men, old and young. *Platinum frequent flier, phenomenal legs, does museums in two hours max* wrote a thirty-six-year-old businesswoman. *Generally a barrel of laughs when not contemplating thoughts of an untimely death* quipped a fortysomething filmmaker. Ginny also enjoyed *Capable of holding entire conversations with answering machines,* and *Rides badly, speaks three foreign languages badly, cooks badly, but does all with vigor & enthusiasm.* She sometimes thought of pairing up two ads with each other: *Zero maintenance* having sushi with *Non-needy seeks other non-needy.* Her affection was stirred by the fellow who claimed to *appreciate all manner of candor*—he was seeking a mate with *poise, wit, and joie de vivre. There is no such thing as too much information,* another single-ton declared. Ginny laughed; she loved that. Her friends found the personals to be categorically depressing, but Ginny had developed a near-obsessive fascination with them, and found in them a source of hope both mundane and profound. *Still trying to chance upon a unified theory of everything, but in the meantime, searching for a soul who is wildly intelligent and in possession of some sadness.* This from an eighty-year-old retired physics professor, who sounded like a winner to Ginny, in spite of the forty-five-year age difference. But by far her favorites were three of the simplest: *Adventuresome, liberal, hair; Got dog?;* and *Good in a crisis.*

Ginny was in no way looking for a mate herself. She described herself as happily married to the single life, and didn't want to be responsible for anyone else's socks or chicken dinners. If she were a plant, her instructions would have read: "Needs ample sunlight; thrives in solitude." Some winter evenings she would turn off her phone, start a fire, open a book—and swear there was no home happier than hers. Her friends called her commitment-phobic to her face, but why label as fear what was simply a choice? When she told them she dreamed of being an old spinster one day, of course no one believed her. But she knew her recent restlessness had little to do with love.

Ginny had no illusions about marriage. To her it looked like boatloads of work and a lifetime of compromise. She realized she was in the minority in her disaffection for the institution; the world was peopled with the betrothed. Still, occasionally her friends confided details that supported her aversion: Jessica's husband, Ted, taped *The X-Files* over their wedding video; Katrina could never cook with her favorite spice, dill, because Leo didn't care for it. And parenthood—parenthood looked like slavery. Ginny found herself newly in awe of her own parents now that her peers had begun to procreate, and she could see up close what was involved. To consider all they had given up—the time, the freedom. "Maybe I'm just too selfish to have children," she confessed to Jessica over the phone.

"Let's not forget, a lot of people *have* children for selfish reasons," Jessica said. "In order to have someone to play with, or to take care of them when they're old. Or because they're bored and don't have anything better to do." Jessica herself was pregnant with baby number four, and Ginny knew her motives were of the more magnanimous variety: She wanted to adore her children in a way she had never been adored.

Truth be told, Ginny already had children—five classes full of them. Despite frustrations, her favorites were the seniors. Twenty seventeen-year-olds were hers for AP English every day, fifth period, right after lunch, when all the blood in their bodies that wasn't already servicing endocrine glands was busy digesting pizza and Gatorade. Nonetheless, she made it her duty to try to love them. And she attempted to impart a few morsels of wisdom; she tried very hard, but more and more she felt that something was being lost on them. She did everything she'd always done: She took them on the field trip to Walden Pond; she read from writers' obituaries; she told them who were the alcoholics, who slept with whom, who were the geniuses and who were the hacks, which one subsisted on a diet of only white wine, oysters, and grapes for so long she had to be hospitalized for anemia. Still, they looked at her with what could only be called accusation. As if she were withholding something. As if there were something that she, Ginny, was supposed to be doing for them, or giving them, but she was simply too selfish or too lazy to do it.

She'd heard of the great teachers who said they learned more from their students than they taught them, so she examined her teenagers' faces with fresh scrutiny and pored over their essays with renewed vigor, wondering what she was supposed to glean. Her kids were so disaffected, so sophisticated, so urbane. A couple of times she could have sworn Marc Campbell had winked at her in the hallway. She had them read *Suite Française,* a World War II novel whose author had perished at Auschwitz while the manuscript was rescued by her daughters. Ginny asked if there were any questions.

"Do you think the sum of the good things mankind has done outweighs the sum of the horrible things?" It was Julia, her star student. Ginny panicked for a second, genuinely stumped, then made up an answer about how it's not always useful to quantify things.

If they wanted difficult questions, she'd give them the difficult questions. "Love is an attempt to penetrate another being, but it can only be realized if the surrender is mutual," she said the following Wednesday. She was reading to them from *The Labyrinth of Solitude* by Octavio Paz. "It is always difficult to give oneself up; few persons anywhere ever succeed in doing so, and even fewer transcend the possessive stage to know love for what it actually is—"

"And you, Miss Porter?" asked Jimmy Galway, interrupting. He was a confusing child: He had the attitude of a tattooed rebel but the fresh-pressed shirts of a diplomat.

"And me what?"

"You one of the few?" It briefly flashed through Ginny's head that she would never have dreamed of interrupting her teachers, never mind daring to ask if they had ever truly succeeded in falling in love. She leaned back against the front of her desk and wished the slit in her slim black skirt stopped an inch lower than it did. But she didn't believe in lying, least of all to the young.

"I have often been in love," she said, matter-of-factly. "But never of the surrendering variety. Or rather, if I do surrender, it doesn't seem to be sustainable for very long." Just then the bell rang, and brought relief. Within the relief, there was also a small pearl of pride, that pleasurable feeling that sometimes accompanies speaking the plain truth.

The pride didn't last. The days dragged; her kids became less and less engaged. Some would unabashedly toy with their cell phones while she was teaching. They didn't do their homework; they chewed gum in glass; Tim Harris sat with an unlit clove cigarette perched on his lips during the entire first act of *Waiting for Godot*. It was as if they were challenging her, calling her out. But she didn't know what was wrong, or how to reach them. Hadn't there been things that had reached her once? Books, films, scraps of beauty that had moved her so deeply she had wept with gratitude? How could she now not remember what they were? Even the well-worn volumes on her own syllabus seemed to have become mere words on a page.

"There's more to life than grammar and spelling," she announced on a rainy Friday afternoon, but it only made them slouch deeper in their chairs, squeaking their sneakers against the linoleum. She felt like a hypocrite. Grammar and spelling, sadly, were her lifeblood. Against her better wishes, she'd become an enforcer of the picayune. Her students must have perceived her failure; with the wisdom of children, they sensed that she had chosen the easy path in life, and they resented her for it.

"I'm sure they don't resent you," Jessica said cheerfully, placing her spoon on the edge of her saucer. All around them, the bright voice of Sam Cooke was greeting itself in the gleaming surfaces of the diner. "They're teenagers. They probably don't give you a second thought. They're too busy thinking about each other, or how to get out of that hellhole." Jessica had so seamlessly made the transition from pink-haired punk rocker to wife and mother that Ginny sometimes forgot about her undying empathy for the disenfranchised.

"That hellhole is my life," Ginny said.

"I know, honey. I'm sorry. I feel for you. You know I do."

"I need to get out of there. It's just—something's got to change," Ginny said. She cupped her mug with both hands. "You know, when I was their age, I loved English class. It was better than honors chemistry with

Mr. Marks. Or writing the Presidents report for Mr. Tully. It was exciting. It was English, with Mr. Hennessey."

Jessica arched an eyebrow. "Mr. Hennessey, the one you were in love with?"

"I wasn't in love with him, I was *inspired* by him. He was my *inspiration*."

"Uh-huh. I thought you said you had your first sex dream about him."

Ginny was grateful she didn't blush easily. "He was my mentor. I mean, all these years, he's been my invisible mentor."

"Why not make him visible?" said Jessica.

"Huh?"

"Why not look him up?"

"Whatever for?" Ginny said, but Jessica only shook her head, slid belly-first out of the booth, and went to pay the check.


Ginny thought about doing a search on the Internet, but in the end, finding Mr. Hennessey was as easy as calling her old high school and speaking to the secretary from whom Ginny used to procure late slips on account of the bus—by God, the same woman still worked there. Arthur Hennessey lived in western Massachusetts now, had stopped teaching ten years ago. His address was 49 Merriam Street, Pittsfield. She had a phone number on file but wasn't sure it was current.

Arthur. It was strange to think of his first name. He'd been, what, maybe thirty-five when she was seventeen?

Which would make him fifty-four now, give or take. She wondered what he'd be doing, why he'd left teaching; it seemed he'd been born to teach. Perhaps he owned a bookstore or had started some sort of nonprofit. Or she could picture him as a ski instructor; he'd always been the chaperone for the school-sponsored ski trips. Would he be married, with a family? He'd been a perennial bachelor back then: tall, dark hair, broad shoulders—practically the bachelor from Central Casting. It was occasionally rumored that he was engaged, or had a girlfriend, but he never seemed to actually get married. He sometimes had a little BO, she remembered, which Ginny's adolescent self had found oddly sexy. Mainly, though, he had the peculiar beauty of a person in love with what he does.

His classroom had all the elegance and electricity hers lacked. He would pepper his lessons with quotes from John Cheever, Walt Whitman, Bob Dylan. He seemed to know something about everything, and he wielded his knowledge not as a weapon but with self-effacing humor and quirkiness. He promised his students two dollars for each time they brought in an example of bad grammar in a pop song—an arrangement that easily could have bankrupted him. Ginny was the first to produce one. "I have a quote from the song 'Hungry Eyes,'" she announced shyly one afternoon. She didn't have to say what it was. "I feel the magic between you and I!" Mr. Hennessey blurted out, as if he were removing a painful splinter from his heel.

He didn't draw the same boundaries her other teachers did. He told them what books he was reading, what movies he liked, what happened the week he was out on jury duty. "We were seated around a large table, and the lawyer questioning potential jurors said: 'Each of you needs to choose which of these adjectives best describes you: leader or follower.' 'Leader,' reported the first. 'Leader,' said the next." Then it was Mr. Hennessey's turn. "Well, if these two are leaders, I'd better be a follower," he said. "But I should inform you, these words are nouns, not adjectives."

He had them memorize and recite their favorite poem. He said he would bring in his guitar and accompany them, if they wanted to sing it. The students laughed, but he was serious. "Each of you should make a point of having at least one great poem committed to memory," he said. "In case you ever have to spend some time in prison."

In the spring he missed half a week of school, and the substitute teacher told them his mother had died. When he returned to class on Thursday, he was quieter than usual, but beneath the surface, the old self blazed. He gave them an essay assignment so he could sit at his desk, writing what looked like thank-you notes. "Write a three-page composition, either fiction or nonfiction, that illustrates how fragile yet how durable we are." Ginny wrote something relatively unimaginative about her dog. That afternoon, when she got home from school, she went to her bedroom, locked the door, and cried.

"Never listen to the world," he announced one sunlit morning in the middle of June. It was the last day of school. "The world gives terrible advice. In fact, more often than not, do the exact opposite of what the world says." This was her final memory of the man, her favorite teacher. She couldn't locate him in the crowd at graduation, couldn't find him afterward to tell him about her college choice, thank him for his recommendation. But he had inhabited her consciousness all these years. Of course he had. And now she had his address.


At first it had seemed fitting and adventuresome to drive to his house on a Saturday afternoon, rather than calling ahead. *The world gives terrible advice,* she repeated to herself, speeding along the MassPike. What kind of advice would Mr. Hennessey give? But now, sitting on the side of the road with the engine still running, she felt ridiculous. She was about a mile from the house, had driven by twice, seen a truck, seen the light on in the kitchen, and kept going. It was October, and both sides of the dirt road were lined with trees whose yellow leaves had already fallen. She knew her students were out at soccer matches and football games, and in the silence she heard their shouts and cheers. While here she sat on a country road, where not a single car had passed her. One minute she was prepared to go back to the house; the next she was ready to drive the two-plus hours it would take to get home. *This must be what a midlife crisis feels like,* she said to herself. Then she remembered *Good in a crisis,* from the personal ads, and laughed. The next thing she knew, she had pulled into his driveway, turned off the engine, and was slamming the car door.

The house was modest and unremarkable. Greenish paint, beige shutters, a few shrubs along the front. An old-fashioned black mailbox hung beside the door. The truck in the driveway was rusted, and the word TOYOTA across its back was missing its final *A,* rendering it a palindrome. Ginny rang the bell and waited, feeling a bit queasy, preparing herself for a wife or child to answer, or a stranger—perhaps this was an old address—anything. She rang the bell again. A moment later, there he was. Mr. Hennessey.

"Yes?" he said through the screen door. She could tell he didn't recognize her. She wore her blond hair long and curly now, and her face had settled in a way that gave her cheekbones she hadn't had when she was seventeen. She was wearing jeans and a brown suede jacket, and carrying an oversize handbag that she thought of as her schoolmarm's purse.

"Mr. Hennessey, hello. It's Virginia Porter. I was a student of yours."

"Virginia Porter," Mr. Hennessey said, a smile widening his face. "Come on in. How the heck are you?"

"I'm all right. I'm a teacher myself now," she said, wishing she'd waited a little longer to say it.

"No kidding! Are you really?" He opened the hall closet. "Here, let me take your coat." If he was shocked to see her, he showed no sign of it. He spoke as though they did this every third Saturday in October.

She pulled her arms out of her jacket, and he helped her. "I am," she said, trying not to grin. She was surprised at how good she felt. Mr. Hennessey's face had surprised her—it had more lines, but it was the same face.

"Have a seat. Do you feel like coffee or anything? Tea?"

"Tea would be great."

The two of them sat on a worn leather sofa opposite a beautifully carved coffee table, holding their cups of tea. Ginny commented on the table, which featured a landscape of seraphs and Cyrillic letters under a sheet of glass.

"I made it," Mr. Hennessey said. "I meant to sell it to someone, but then I ended up keeping it. Funny how things work out sometimes."

"You're a natural—it's gorgeous. Is that what you do these days, woodwork?"

"I do a bunch of things; handyman stuff, mostly. I have some friends with farms who do a lot of canning, so there's seasonal work. It suits me; I like being outdoors. It's nice out here."

"What made you give up teaching?" Ginny said, not realizing until she asked it how the question had been pressing on her. "You were so great at it."

"You don't know?" Mr. Hennessey said, adjusting his position. "It was quite the scandal back in the day. I thought everyone knew."

Ginny felt her face go hot, ashamed both that she didn't know and that she might have brought up an indelicate topic. "I guess I'm behind the times. I never heard a thing."

"Oh. Well. It was six or seven years after your class. On a ski trip, one of the boys was arrested for smoking pot. Just one of those kid things. No harm done, really. He and his friends had taken a bag to the top of the mountain, presumably to get high and then ski down. But since the trip was in Canada and they'd carried it across the U.S. border, it became a big deal. The authorities pressed him about who sold it to him, and the kid said I had. Said I gave him the weed earlier that day. That everyone knew I would supply students with drugs—all they had to do was ask.

"It was entirely made up, of course, probably out of desperation. But the school board took it rather seriously, as you can imagine. They searched my house, depositioned me. In the end I was vindicated, but after that, it was as if the wind had gone out of my sails. A year later I left."

"I'm so sorry," Ginny said. "I didn't know any of this. I didn't know a thing."

"Don't be sorry. It all turned out for the best. I like it here. I have plenty of time to read. And it's quiet. Peaceful."

Ginny surveyed the room—the crowded bookshelves, the dusty white curtains, the guitar case in the corner next to an expensive-looking stereo. It did seem like the abode of a contented person. Simple but homey.

He lifted his teacup. "What about you?" he said. "How do you like your life?"

"My life is generally a barrel of laughs when I'm not contemplating thoughts of an untimely death," she said, which she'd hoped would make him laugh, but it didn't. "I like my life all right," she said, and found herself wishing they were drinking beer rather than tea. She remembered the restaurant in Chinatown that was the only place in Boston where you could get alcohol after serving hours, by ordering a kettle of "cold tea." Cold tea, wink wink.

"Anything exciting going on?" he said. "Where do you teach?"

"Lexington High School," she said. "English. I even have the AP class."

"Ah!" Mr. Hennessey said. "Our archrivals! How could you?"

"It's just the way the numbers worked out. It's nothing personal," she said, as if she were a professional ballplayer.

"And forgive me if I was hoping you'd say English rather than chemistry."

Ginny made a snort. "All I remember from chemistry is Avogadro's number. And even that I don't remember."

"Avogadro isn't worth remembering. Unless you're out on a date with a chemist you want to impress."

"I guess that explains why that one never called again," she said. She found her gaze shifting to Mr. Hennessey's hands. There was no wedding band; there was no evidence of children's things around the house.

"How about you?" she said. "Dating any chemists?"

"No."

"Did you ever marry?"

Mr. Hennessey put down his cup of tea. "No."

"Why not?"

He looked at her. He'd always encouraged his students to be candid and direct, and his expression implied he was pleased that someone had finally taken him up on it.

"Just not for me, I suppose."

"I know what you mean," Ginny said. "I feel that way about eggplant."

Mr. Hennessey clicked his tongue. "Now that's a pity. That means you won't be able to sample my beer-battered fried eggplant extraordinaire."

"I hope you're kidding," Ginny said. "Wow, you're

serious? How about just a beer, minus the eggplant extraordinaire."

Mr. Hennessey rose to his feet. "All right, Virginia," he said. "But it's your loss."

Two beers later, she was feeling much more relaxed. Mr. Hennessey had put on a Tom Waits CD, and Ginny thought he had the saddest yet most hopeful voice she'd ever heard.

"Mr. Hennessey, would you mind if I asked you a question?"

"On one condition: You have to stop calling me Mr. Hennessey. You make me feel as if it's still 1987. We need to bring ourselves up to date."

Ginny offered her hand. "Deal," she said. She took a breath. "Arthur, do you think the good things human beings have done outweigh the hideous things?"

Mr. Hennessey nearly spilled his beer. "What the hell kind of question is that?"

"The kind my kids ask. That's from Julia, who's an ace, but so shy. She writes these ingenious paragraphs about the overlooked dross of the world, but never makes a peep in class. Then the other day she finally spoke up, and I let her down. I couldn't help her," Ginny said. "It was awful."

"I'll tell you what I think: It only takes one moment of perfection to atone for a lifetime of waste."

Ginny sat up as if he'd slapped her. "Perfection? I beg your pardon? Aren't you the man whose blackboard perennially read: *Strive for perfection, but learn to work with imperfection*? You taught us perfection was a chimera. I thought it was a fiction."

"So did I," he said. "But I was wrong. Perfection isn't outside us. Perfection is a way of seeing."

Ginny fell silent. *You were less cryptic before you became enlightened,* she wanted to say, but the lines on his face appeared freshly earnest, as if each were the receipt for some suffering, and she changed her mind. Mr. Hennessey split the caps off two fresh bottles and handed her one. She thought about declining, not certain what it would mean in terms of her drive home, but she accepted, and clinked her bottle to his.

"To perfection," she said.

"To 1987," said Mr. Hennessey.


While Mr. Hennessey was in the bathroom, Ginny realized she was drunk. It felt good; it felt as if she'd needed to get drunk for a long time.

"Personally, I think the whole endeavor is overrated," she said as he reclaimed his place beside her.

"Which endeavor is that?"

"Life. The pursuit of happiness. Love."

"Is that so."

"That is definitely so. I swear by it. My kids, for example. My class. They're so suspicious and disengaged. I think they sense something insincere in me, and they hate it. They hate my class."

"*Is* there something insincere in you?"

"No. Well, yes. I mean, teaching. I'm not sure I want to be a teacher anymore."

The words hung in the air; Mr. Hennessey didn't seem to have a response. "I'm sorry," she said. "I didn't mean to burden you with all this stuff. I just thought you might have some advice."

He leaned back against the couch. "Tell me," he said. "What do you think will become of Julia?" She didn't blame him for changing the subject; she hadn't meant to dump her life in his lap.

"I don't know. She's so sensitive, I worry. I think either she'll have to toughen up, or the world will toughen her up." Ginny had noticed that people didn't seem to value sensitivity much. "Don't be so sensitive!" they'd shout— not the most delicate way to handle a finely attuned person—as if sensitivity were voluntary.

He smiled. "Or not."

"What do you mean?"

"Maybe she'll find a way to capitalize on her sensitivity."

"I doubt it."

"Why's that?"

"I just do." Ginny thought about the way Julia's hands shook when it was her turn to read aloud, how the skin on her arms turned to gooseflesh whenever she read a sentence that was especially moving.

"You don't think it could ever be an asset—perhaps her greatest asset?"

"No." Ginny laughed. "I don't."

Mr. Hennessey gave her a funny look. *Interesting*, his

expression said. "Would you mind if I asked you a personal question?"

"That'd be only fair."

"What was your poem? When I had the students memorize their favorite poem and recite it."

"Oh, God, I don't remember. That was so long ago. I couldn't begin to remember."

He smiled an enigmatic smile she didn't appreciate. He was sitting only a foot away, and she found herself partly wanting to scoot over next to him and partly wanting to reach for her purse and flee.

He leaned forward and set his bottle down on the table. "Well, I'd say if you truly don't enjoy teaching, you should leave. But if you do enjoy it, you should stay. Personally, I can't picture you as anything other than an excellent teacher."

"But—I'm not like you. I'm not the way you were."

"You're like yourself," he said. "Even better."

"You don't know me," she said, becoming annoyed, wishing she hadn't accepted that last beer. Or was it that she felt as if she were only seventeen again? Her father had taken her aside that year, told her he was worried about her, that she was like a turtle without a shell. "You don't know me," she said again. "I toughened up. I grew a shell. I'm not—"

He put his hand against her back but, oddly, she felt it in her stomach. "Your shell is papier-mâché," he said. "You are a piñata."

She looked into his face. It was still so handsome. *You were my favorite teacher,* she wanted to say, but she was too embarrassed, too afraid she would sound like a schoolgirl with a crush. *You were everybody's favorite.*

He held her eyes. "And I'm no good at being in love, either," she said abruptly, shifting away from him. She sometimes had a talent for dispelling awkward moments by making them even more awkward. "I don't like the idea of giving yourself up, of surrendering. Why does it have to be like that? Who invented this system, anyway?"

Mr. Hennessey appeared stunned, and she wondered if she'd scared him.

"Did you put truth serum in my drink?" she said, hoping to recover a little. But he had grown pensive. For the first time, she recognized the expression she knew from the classroom.

"I don't know that you necessarily have to give yourself up," he said. "Maybe your self just becomes larger."

"Spoken like a lifelong bachelor," she said, but when she saw his face, she regretted it.

"I was engaged once," he said, turning to the window. Outside, the sun was setting, and the western sky was the colors of a bruise: purple and yellow, fading to gray. "She was curious about everything. And what a heart." As he spoke, the room seemed quiet in a way it hadn't before. Ginny sat perfectly still.

"Her name was Isabel," he said. "When she left, it took something from me. Changed me. I almost feel as if I've been in hibernation. For a while, I suppose I was waiting for her to come back. But at a certain point, I imagine one's supposed to give up." His face had a vulnerability she'd never seen in it when he was her teacher. "I guess I just never knew when to give up."

He seemed about to say more, but then he stopped. He pressed his lips together. *If I see this man cry,* Ginny thought, *it will break me. If I see him cry, I will break in two.* But instead of attempting to say more, he just smiled—a broad, apologetic smile—as if he were laughing at his own predicament, at how funny it was to have been through such heartache.

"That was five or six years ago now," he said, sitting up. "The interesting thing is, I stayed friends with her father. He lived right up the road. I used to go over and help him out with repair-type stuff around the house, things he was too weak to do himself. Sometimes we'd just sit and talk. But we never mentioned Isabel. One day, one of the last times I saw him before he died, he looked at me and said: 'Arthur, God answered all my prayers. All my prayers in life—except for one.' I knew he was trying to help me."

Ginny didn't know what to say. She wanted to help him, too, but she didn't know how. She felt terrible then, terrible that she was considering leaving teaching, terrible that she was such a failure.

"I'm sorry if I let you down," she said softly.

Mr. Hennessey shook his head. "You didn't let me down. You could never let me down." He lifted her chin. "You were my Julia," he said. "You were my quiet ace."

Ginny closed her eyes. " 'Suddenly I realize that if I stepped out of my body I would break into blossom,' " she said, and kept her eyes shut, afraid to open them, afraid of everything.

"James Wright's 'A Blessing.' Of course. That would be the perfect poem for you," he said. Then he leaned in and kissed her, respectful and slow at first, then in a way that let her feel his hunger. She kissed him back, raising her hand to his neck. The simple act of touching him with tenderness made the hair on her arms stand up.

When they stopped kissing, he pulled her into a hug, both arms locking her against his body, tight. Then they both started to laugh—real, deep laughter—and the more they laughed, the more they wanted to laugh. It was as if they had just heard the funniest joke in the world. It was as if they *were* the funniest joke in the world. When they stopped laughing, Ginny felt as if she might start to cry again. She stared at the vertical row of buttons on his shirt.

"I can't remember what I used to think was beautiful," she said.

"You're beautiful," he whispered. "You just might be the most beautiful thing."

"You're drunk," Ginny laughed. "And insane. Both." But her giddiness quickly evaporated. She didn't want to hurt him, not Mr. Hennessey, not this great, invisible love of her life.

"I should get going," she said, releasing him and glancing at her watch.

"I'm not sure you're medically fit to drive," he said. "Besides, I was just about to offer you the guest room, and suggest we make pancakes tomorrow morning, then lounge around all day reading books."

"Reading books, eh?"

"Or engaging in stimulating activity of one fashion or another."

Ginny smiled. "I told you, I'm no good at the love thing."

"I'm willing to wager you're better than you think. And who said anything about love? I said pancakes."

She stalled for a moment. She knew she should leave. She knew her pattern, her tendency to leave a broken heart in her wake when she returned to her solitary ways.

"Arthur—"

"Stay."

She reached for her purse. "I can't. I'm sorry. I really have to go." She started for the door.

He took her arm. "Wait," he said. He drew a breath. "I do miss it. I miss every damn thing about it. I should never have left. It was ego, pride. I'm envious of you," he said. "I'm jealous."

Ginny sat down, shocked. "What? That's insane. Why don't you go back, teach again somewhere? You could start fresh."

He was shaking his head. "It's not that simple," he said. "I've been away for so long. Sometimes you can miss something even when you know it's not for you anymore."

"That's a load of bull. You were a fantastic teacher. You could get a job again in an instant. Heck, you can have my job. You just have to teach me how to carve tables."

"Classes could be arranged," he said, taking her hand.

She slipped her hand away. The clock on the wall read 8:35. The alcohol was wearing off, and she suddenly felt very tired.

"I really should leave," she said.

"Fair enough," he said, and they both stood up. Then he kissed her again, and it was as sweet as before. When she opened her eyes, his pupils were wide.

"Hold on—I'll be right back," he said. "I think I still have something you'll get a huge kick out of." Then he headed up the stairs, taking them two at a time.

While he was gone, Ginny scanned the room, her eyes lighting on the bookshelves, the stereo, the coffee table. For a moment, she took in the whole scene, herself included, as if viewing it from above. She laughed. She knew then that she would leave teaching; she could see how much it had been misplaced admiration for him all along. And she imagined with equal clarity the possibility that he would return to it. She could see the strands of their lives crisscrossing like two chromosomes.

Outside, the sun had fully set, and a few lights glimmered through the clouds. Somewhere in the darkness a dog barked, and she heard a screen door slam. Ginny took her purse, and without making a sound, went for the door. All of her instincts told her to vanish, to flee. All of her instincts, except for one. The next minute, she was climbing the stairs—very slowly, like a woman sleepwalking, incapable of imagining the dream that awaits her when she wakes up.

# THE THING ITSELF

Something was about to happen. He could feel it. He could feel it with the same eerie certainty he used to have in his school days, when he would know, a millisecond before it happened, whether his bat was going to connect with the ball. He could feel it the way he would occasionally dream of an old friend the day before he received a letter from him; the way he once suddenly understood, watching his mother's car stop at the curb of his school at three o'clock, that his dog had run away again, this time for good. The way, years later, pursuing his favorite hobby, he knew without prior word from his library that Harris's *The Art of Astonishment* had arrived, and he could drop in on his way home and claim it for the weekend. The way he'd always known a rainy evening in a cloudless day.

Its precise dimensions eluded him. There was simply an amorphous excitement, a peripheral tingling that had begun to pervade his waking hours, making it difficult for him to sleep. And when he did sleep, even his dreams were harbingers. They'd become vivid and strange. Never comprehensible, at least not in describable terms, they left a residual scent on his skin—his body, when he awoke, had the faintly metallic sweetness that used to clothe him after hours spent outdoors as a child. How strange that he should awake smelling as if he'd been playing all day in the woods outside Durham, New Hampshire—a place he hadn't visited in more than thirty years.

Such premonitions used to frighten him. Once he seemed to know in advance that he was going to be mugged. He'd just taken a job with the new firm, and for a week he felt overly aware of strangers in his personal space. On a whim, he decided to photocopy the contents of his wallet, although he couldn't have said why. He thought about asking Daphne, the paralegal who wore low-cut blouses and black fingernail polish, to do it for him. But he'd concluded it was more prudent to do it himself. That night, on the way from his favorite restaurant to his car, he was cornered in the parking lot by a hooded man with a knife. Even as he surrendered the calf-skin billfold, he couldn't help thinking, with a dark pride: *I knew it!*

But he was a man of logic, not superstition. He was a lawyer. True, he was a lawyer in Los Angeles, but still, there were certain standards. He didn't think he possessed ESP. On the contrary, he wondered if these weren't instances of SSP: subtle sensory perception. Possibly the mugger had been casing him throughout the week, and he'd noticed him subconsciously. Perhaps the old friend had called, and left no message, but he'd seen the name flash by his caller ID. Maybe he'd glimpsed a smudge of tears on his mother's face, or had seen a dog collar or some other token in her steering-wheel hand. There were always explanations for things, if you looked hard enough.

Or so he told himself. Unheeding, his heart beat back its answer: Something was coming. And soon.

"You mean, like the way you know when you're about to sneeze?" Daphne said, crossing her legs on her side of the booth at Bandera. She was wearing black leather boots that laced up to her knees. She'd been an aspiring actress, and still had the clothes.

"Sort of like that," he said. It was possible that telling her had been a mistake. On an impulse, he'd chosen her as the person in whom to confide; she seemed more open to paranormal exotica than his friends. He needed to tell someone, and he couldn't tell his wife. His wife's parents had died in a plane crash when she was in high school. When she and he were first dating, in the mid-nineties, she'd become pregnant and had had an abortion. Then, when they married several years later, she hadn't been able to conceive. Now they were both in their forties, and she more than he was haunted by the one child they seemingly could have had, the gift they'd thrown away. She had little tolerance for talk of "premonitions."

He lifted his glass, then put it down. "It feels sort of like déjà vu," he said. "Except in reverse."

"I'm not sure I know what that means," Daphne said, and he realized she had a point. She sat staring into her globe of merlot, her handsome face catching its scarlet refractions. Was she disappointed she'd never made it as an actress? She was probably in her late thirties—though he'd always had difficulty telling ages—but her heart-shaped face and little-girl voice made her seem younger. If having to give up her dreams had broken her spirit, she didn't show it.

"Unless—do you mean like feeling nostalgic for a place you've never been?" she said.

"Yes," he said. "More like that."

She reached for her purse, a red suede thing with fringes. "Would you like me to read your cards? I have a Tarot deck in here somewhere."

"No, thanks," he said quickly. He was feeling burdened enough by his own presentiments; he didn't need do-it-yourself prophecy added to the mix.

Daphne's hands stopped their rummaging. "I'm not sure how I can help you then, Felix."

"I don't need help, exactly. I just thought I should tell someone." The roots of his hair prickled with sweat. He knew how they must look to passersby: an overweight, balding, nervous-seeming lawyer sitting across from a lithe, semi-Goth paralegal at a steakhouse three blocks from their office. "The last time this happened, I was mugged," he said.

"So you think you're about to be mugged?" she said, snapping the thin thread of understanding he'd hoped was being spun between them. In the two years she'd been working at his firm, she had occasionally entered his fantasies, but he'd never before had the temerity to ask her to join him for an after-work drink.

"No," he said, staring at his untouched gimlet. "It's not that. It's more . . ." He struggled for a way to explain the sense of urgency he felt like a rising tide in his blood. "It's more like this bumper sticker I saw on the back of an eighteen-wheeler." He found himself thinking of the tailpipe slogan several times a day; it cropped up, unbidden, in myriad idle moments.

"That said what?"

"'After a rolling ball comes a running child.'"

She looked at him. Her eyes were smudged with black, like a raccoon's, and for a second she reminded him of the way his wife used to look, when she was younger, after one of her crying jags.

"Sounds like a line from a poem," she said. She pulled a compact from her purse and began to refresh her lipstick.

"No—don't you see?" he said, shifting in his seat. He tugged at the collar of his shirt. "It's a warning. It's meant to warn people, so something terrible doesn't happen."

Daphne appeared bored and irritated. Her cell phone chirped, and he wondered if she'd somehow willed it to do so. She read the text message eagerly, then slid a ten-dollar bill under her wineglass.

"It's my boyfriend," she said. "I've got to go."

Janet was brushing her teeth. Felix was sitting on the edge of the bed, still in his jacket and bow tie. He looked handsome in bow ties, had since he was a kid. They'd just come from an office party, where he'd had several seltzer waters—lately he felt it necessary to remain clearheaded at all times—and she'd had enough wine that the little chapped patches of skin on her lips had gone purple.

"I think the new partner likes you," he said.

Janet spat in the sink, ran the water. "What makes you say that?"

"I can just tell."

"That's not a bad thing, is it?"

"No." He undid his tie, still sitting. For some reason he lacked the will to stand up and undress. After a moment, Janet flushed the toilet. She emerged from the bathroom and slid next to him on the bed. She seemed happier than usual. At the party, an associate had been trying to convince her to get an iPod, saying there were so many scholarly podcasts on the Web, it was a shame not to have access to them during her long commute. Especially someone like her, who worked in research, and liked to keep up-to-date.

"You seem to like info," he'd said.

"Oh, I'm an info maniac!" Janet had said, not hearing how it sounded until it was too late. Then her face had contorted, and the whole group had erupted with laughter.

"You know, there are treatments for that now," said the new partner, dabbing at his eyes with his napkin. "Perhaps Felix could help you out with that." Then they'd all laughed again, Felix with his hand at the small of his wife's back.

Beside him on the bed, she leaned over and kissed his neck, then bit the end of his loosened tie and pulled it off with her teeth. She smiled at him with the thing still in her mouth, like a puppy. She looked ridiculous—and cute. He knew there'd been times she'd thought of leaving him. After the failed fertility treatments, for a while they'd both avoided sex, and he'd wondered if it might be forever tainted with a subtle ache, the memory of failure. The failure was difficult to forget, not least because they'd never refurnished the nursery. Janet's therapist had advised her to make room for a child in her life, to visualize and prepare, to attract success by assuming success. So Felix had refinished an old mahogany sleigh crib that had been his father's, and Janet had bought onesies, babybjörns, and a rocking-chair's worth of stuffed bunnies, lambs, and giraffes at stores with names like Babycakes and Little One. They'd even had a local artist decorate the walls with scenes from their favorite nursery rhymes in low-fume paints. On one wall stood a little match girl whose hair and tiny flame were the same color as the whorls of stars on the ceiling—a silvery butter. In the end, neither of them had had the heart to take it all away, paint over the stars. So they just kept the door closed, à la Miss Havisham.

She was unbuttoning his shirt. Her hands dropped to his belt. The cheerful speediness of her movements stilled and excited him. He kissed her forehead as she worked off his shoes. He hadn't seen her like this in a long time. Maybe it was the wine; he made a mental note to ask the host for the vintage.


Afterward, she curled away on her side of the bed, the sheet up to her chin. He moved over and put his hands on her shoulders. They were quavering.

"Janet," he said.

She kept sobbing. "I'm sorry," she said, without turning around. Her voice sounded strange and faraway.

He took his hands off her. "For what?" he said.

"I was reading this book and it said: 'When you don't forgive someone, it's like drinking poison and expecting someone else to die.'" She wiped her nose with the sheet. "But what if the person you can't forgive is yourself?"

He exhaled. For a second he'd thought he was about to hear her confess to an affair, potentially ending his marriage and his premonitions in the same breath. Instead it was just the old pain, rearing its graying head. Their pain was aging along with them.

"Then forgive yourself," he said.

She reached for a Kleenex. "I don't think it's that simple."

"Sure it is," he said, taking her hands. "I, Felix, forgive thee, Janet." He waited. "Now it's your turn to forgive you."

"You know I hate it when you get like this," she said, but there was a smile in her voice.

He pulled her hands behind her back. "Say it," he said. "Like you mean it. Or I'll keep you as my prisoner forever."

She started to speak, but as soon as she opened her mouth, her eyes filled again. He felt her body go limp. Then, a moment later, she did it.

"I forgive you, Janet," she said quietly, barely breathing the words.

He drew her into an embrace. "You can still be my prisoner," he said into her hair. Then he released her and looked at her seriously. "We need to redo the nursery," he said.


Things were good between them for the next few weeks. But Felix had a secret, and Janet was catching on. Why was he keeping a tape recorder under his pillow at night? How come he kept calling in sick to work when he wasn't really sick? What was making him so edgy? He told her the tape recorder was in case something came to him in a dream. Janet laughed. As if the illogic of dreams were worth remembering. He explained that work had become stressful and boring—if it was possible to be stressful and boring at the same time—and that his stomach really had been bothering him. Janet looked him over and said she knew what he needed. He needed a vacation.

The plan was to go snorkeling off San Diego, stay in a bed-and-breakfast, eat clam shooters and drink white wine, sleep till noon. It was not as relaxing as it sounds. It was bad enough to be on an airplane when you felt Something Big was about to happen, but the baritone in the row behind them was some sort of amateur earthquake enthusiast. At one point Felix balled up bits of his cocktail napkin and stuck them in his ears. Janet turned away. After she finished her Bloody Mary she began folding her empty peanuts bag into smaller and smaller triangles. Finally she said, "Is that so you won't have to talk to me?"

Once they were settled, he was less at home in the ocean than was Pisces Janet, and at one point swallowed so much water through his snorkel that he coughed for twenty minutes. He'd always thought snorkeling—the renting of mouthpieces hundreds of other people had mouthed—was disgusting, like eating bowling shoes. But Janet seemed determined to get her money's worth, so he swam along, one eye on her black bikini (she could compete with any twenty-five-year-old), and the other eye scanning the periphery for barracudas and sharks.

At dinner they both ordered the mahi mahi, and as soon as the waiter was out of sight, she stared him down.

"What," she said, "is going on with you?"

"Nothing," he said. He saw little bulbs of muscle at her jawline tense.

"You do realize there are all kinds of betrayals in a marriage," she said. "Screwing the neighbor's wife isn't the only one." A gull cawed in the distance, and she turned to the ocean. "You used to tell me everything," she said.

He sat perfectly still. She was right. He'd told her things he'd never told another living soul, things he knew she'd take with her to her grave. When they were first dating, they used to sleep together on his twin bed, and they could have fit two more people.

But there was no way to explain this to her. After his mother, Janet was the most practical woman he'd ever met. She would laugh him out of the restaurant. She would think less of him.

"It's a surprise," he said. "You'll see. You won't want to have known in advance."

"I'd rather not be surprised," Janet said, unswaddling her knife and fork from their napkin.

The waiter arrived with the appetizers. "Well, you're going to have to be," said Felix.

Back in their room, Janet stuck to her side of the bed and immediately went to sleep. All night long, while she slept beside him, he stared at the ceiling fan, as alert as if the cashews he'd eaten from the minibar had been fistfuls of espresso beans. The red numerals on the alarm clock seemed to quiver with life. *Something's coming,* they said.

The Monday he got back, the head of the firm called him into his office. "We had a problem while you were away," he said. Felix felt a percussive rhythm in his chest. "Hackers got into our system. I'll need you to draft a letter to all your clients explaining what has happened. And you should expect an internal audit of all your accounts."

In his head, Felix began scanning his data banks for possible humiliations. As unpleasant as it was to contemplate his boss reading every personal e-mail he'd ever written, he hadn't done anything objectionable. At least, nothing he could think of. But he didn't really want to think about it too much. Instead, he went into his office, closed the door, and began to work on the letter.

While he set out to make a list of his cases with the most sensitive confidential information, that wasn't the list he found himself composing.

| | |
|---|---|
| Bartlett v. Johnson | *vindictiveness, lying* |
| Crump v. Orozco | *stinginess, stonewalling* |
| Mykytiuk v. Hydratia | *greed, negligence, subsequent lying* |

One of his most important clients was a company that was spending more money defending its toxic dumping than it would have cost to clean it up. He laid down his mechanical pencil and stared at the page. He didn't recall having written the final three words, but there they were: *I hate this.*

At the end of the week, he went to Bandera. Janet didn't expect him until late on Fridays, and Bandera was always crowded in a way that made him feel part of the throng rather than separate from it. Not that he would have minded being alone. By this point, the anticipation had escalated to a low-frequency ringing in his ears, and after a long day, he sometimes had difficulty understanding what people were saying.

Tonight it was the opposite of when he'd come with Daphne. It seemed he couldn't drink enough. He ordered a gimlet, then a vodka tonic, then a martini. He was hoping to discover the elixir that would clear his mind, sober him up. Nothing did. It was a mistake to have admitted to himself that he hated his work, and now that he had, he couldn't take it back. He could see with painful clarity how he'd wound up in this predicament. He'd enjoyed the study of law, but the practice of law had less to do with John Rawls and more to do with filing BlueBacks. Law school had been the classic intellectual sanctuary from certain practical considerations. Then it had ended, and he'd needed to make a living. So here he was.

When he was young, perhaps because of the premonitions, he'd wanted to be a magician. In a box somewhere in his mother's attic there was even a photograph of him in a peach tuxedo, holding a black hat and a pack of cards, grinning. As a teenager, he'd told his secret ambition to his mother, a woman who lived as if she'd come of age in the Great Depression rather than the 1950s. "Dreamer," she'd muttered, under her breath. But Felix had heard. Some mornings he wondered if he'd become a lawyer precisely because it was the least dreamlike thing he could be.

There was Daphne. She was sitting at the other end of the bar, with what must have been her boyfriend, a surprisingly preppy-looking guy in a St. John's lacrosse shirt. Felix rose and ambled toward her, sliding his glass along the polished brass countertop.

"Hello, Miss Edmunds," he said. He could see the lacy outline of a black bra through her blouse. "And how are you this evening?"

"Bug off, buddy," said the boyfriend.

Felix was eager to correct the impression that he was a suitor. "We work together," he said. He thought, but did not say: *I'm her boss.*

"Whoop dee do," said the boyfriend. Daphne was plucking a cherry off a toothpick with her dark fingernails. "Leave her alone," he said. "You're not her type."

Felix looked at Daphne. The minx lifted her shoulders and let them fall, as if to say: *You're not; what can we do?*

Of all the— "Look, pal," Felix said, straightening to his full height.

The boyfriend laughed. "Look? Yeah? Look where?"

Felix checked himself. It wasn't worth it. None of it was worth it. He walked back to his stool and grabbed his coat, tapping his forehead in a quick salute.

"See you 'round," he said.

He was too drunk to drive, too agitated to sit still in a cab. So he decided to walk. As he swayed his way up the freeway on-ramp, he realized why no one walks in Los Angeles. All these drivers, swerving and honking, in a hurry and angry about it! It was as if they were all late for somewhere they didn't want to be going in the first place. Why didn't they just go somewhere better?

Then it hit him. That's what he would do. He would change his life. It wasn't too late. He had money in the bank; Janet had a good job; he didn't have to sit at a desk growing bitter like Daphne—clearly she was more bitter than he'd first imagined. He could switch careers, take a risk—he wouldn't have to become a magician, but he could do something he enjoyed more than practicing law. Heck, at this point, almost anything would satisfy that criterion. He picked up his pace. He felt more sure-footed. Maybe this thing wasn't something that would happen *to* him so much as something he would initiate *himself*.

But he needed a plan. A plan was paramount. He pressed his fingers to his temples and tried to think. The driver of a red Taurus threw an empty Pepsi bottle out the window, and it nicked his elbow. Felix didn't care. The world, like a bride, was finally unveiling its hidden mysteries to him. He had a friend who was opening a bar and had asked him to look over the paperwork. Perhaps

Felix could go in on it with him, be his partner, make it a place like Bandera. Or maybe he could start a restaurant that also had a cabaret in the back, for musicians and actors, even magicians.

He was smiling and his heart was beating fast. It was possible he'd found the perfect solution. When he got home, he would open up and tell Janet everything. She might not like his idea at first, but she would come around—she always did. He would kiss her on the lips while she was still asleep, then he would turn on the bedside lamp and explain to her that change was possible. Change, life, all of it. The dream of his youth was not entirely dead. There was a flicker of something true that burned within him still. It was a relief to realize such a thing. No, it was victory. It was the thing itself.

Someone yelled something and waved his arm out the window. Felix ignored it. A feeling he recognized from childhood had crept into his chest and was radiating out his skin. He felt free for the first time in decades; it was as if the air he'd been inhaling up till now had all been made of counterfeit oxygen. Tomorrow morning he would quit his job, then he would call his mother and ask her to look for that picture of him in the peach tuxedo. Life could still be an adventure. It wasn't too late. Cars whizzed past him, but he didn't even notice them anymore. His eyes were fixed on the moon, full and low and lovely, like a beacon. Like a rolling ball of white light in the sky.

It all happened so quickly it was hard to feel anything except surprise. He got home and closed the door quietly; he didn't want to disturb Janet. He stepped inside, feeling stealth and tiny, like an ant that had just completed a long journey. But as soon as he crossed the threshold, there she was, standing in the foyer, her eyes glossy with a happiness he'd never seen in them before. As if she'd been waiting for him. As if his adventure were just about to start.

# THE LAZIEST FORM

# OF REVELATION

I'm wearing only my underpants and sitting in a window seat with my back to the Hasidic grocery across the street. It's one in the afternoon, and Misha is painting me. The embroidered cushion on which my backside rests was initially a comfort, but over the course of the past four hours, with the help of the midday sun, it has begun to feel like a very subtle instrument of torture. Inexplicably, it is itching me in a way I feel in my gut. There are those who spend their lives consciously or unconsciously courting such discomforts; I am not one of them. Something about Misha's style makes him try to capture as much as possible of the final painting in the initial sitting, so I'm essentially on a twelve-hour fourth-date semi-naked marathon. At first I thought this arrangement might be enlightening, if not downright conducive to epiphanies— the endurance, the inner quiet, the lack of food. But thus far, the experience is more sweaty than transcendent.

"What are you working on?" I ask. Misha is silent, but I can see the color on the tip of his brush. "Are you doing my hair? My mane?"

"It's a complicated red," he says half-distractedly, like a combination painter-oenophile.

"Thank you," I say. Misha says nothing. "I get it from my grandmother."

He shifts his weight to his other foot. "Is it the reason for your name?"

"God, no. I was bald when I was born. That's just an unfortunate coincidence." I then proceed to tell him the story of my paternal grandmother, Florence—"Torchy," they called her in college—whose hair was so red that as a little girl, she wasn't allowed to sit as close to the fire as her sisters were. Her mother was afraid her head would ignite out of sympathy with the flames. Misha seems to like this story.

"Okay," I say. "Now you have to tell me a story about your grandmother."

He dips his brush and continues painting. "What if I don't have any?" he says. I make a pout, even though I've been instructed to maintain an approximation of equipoise at all times. When he gets to my face (apparently he saves this for last), I won't be allowed to speak.

"Then make one up."

He answers while painting, his eyes fixed on the canvas. "My grandmother was a Jew," he says. "My mother, Zdena, was born inside a concentration camp. Once I asked her how it was possible for an infant to survive in such a place, but she just shook her head, and we never spoke of it again." He utters these words with a perfectly blank expression, in monotone, and I have the strange feeling he isn't making it up at all.

"Is that true?" I say.

He shrugs.

"You shouldn't joke around about things like that."

"Who says I'm joking?" he says, momentarily lifting his focus from the canvas to lock eyes with me. His eyes are as beautiful and opaque as polished stones.

Misha and I met two months ago, when he was walking his dachshund in SoHo. I would later learn that he'd been there to drop off his portfolio at a gallery, and that the dog was on loan from a friend who'd gone home to Ukraine for a week. A blonde in a black fur coat made ooohs of excitement and bent down to pet the animal.

"It's a wiener dog!" she said.

Misha examined her coolly. "'Wiener dog,' madam, is a racial slur."

I was standing nearby, holding my bike, about to text a friend to see if she wanted to join me for coffee. Upon hearing this, I started to laugh. I reached into my backpack and asked if it would be all right if I gave the dog a piece of beef jerky. Thirty minutes later, Misha and I were having espressos at Café Luxe, and I had agreed to go on a date with him. When he told me he was a painter, I think I knew that I would one day consent to sit for him.

It should have dawned on me then how breathtakingly boring it would be. The one saving grace is that Misha is actually quite good. The Marlborough Chelsea recently showed his work, and reviews called his paintings—

especially the oil portraits—extremely accomplished and well-conceived. But what I like is they have an unfinished quality that makes them look alive. Still, in spite of a frequently exercised inner life, I'm restless.

"Let's play a game," I say. Misha takes a sip from a water glass on the stool beside him. "Name something you regret," I say.

He swallows and puts down the glass. "I'm not sure I want to play this game," he says.

"Well, I'm not sure I want to sit here this long."

He appears dissatisfied with whatever he sees on the canvas. "I regret everything," he says.

"Interesting," I say, quietly hoping he doesn't mean anything particular to me or my person. "Name something you're afraid of."

"Falling microwave ovens," he says, then reconsiders. "Cilantro."

"You're afraid of cilantro."

"*Allergic* is probably a better word."

"I see," I say. I'm waiting for him to crack a smile, but he doesn't. "When was the last time you were genuinely happy?"

"I'm always happy," he says.

"Take the game seriously, please. Or I'll be forced to come over there, and sit in your lap, and all will be lost."

He smiles, then thinks for a moment. "Once I was at the seashore with some friends, and we made a fire and drank for many hours and then passed out on the beach. One guy threw up next to my face, and mosquitoes were eating me all night. Meanwhile the tide was coming in around us. I didn't sleep a wink. When the sun came up, it felt like the end of the world—a beautiful end of the world."

"That was when you were last genuinely happy."

"Yes."

"That might be more the European version of happiness than the American one."

He stops painting and examines me. "You doing all right?" he says. "Do you need some water or anything?"

"I'm all right," I say, trying to impress him with my ascetic skills. I ignore a spontaneously itchy kneecap. "Now it's your turn. Ask me anything."

He holds his brush midair, considering. It's impossible to tell whether he's considering my question or the painting. His hair and eyebrows are as black as squid ink, and standing by his easel, staring pensively into the middle distance, he almost looks like a painting himself.

"What are your weaknesses?" he says. This seems an unusual choice, given the panoply of options, but I'm willing to roll with it.

"Physical or metaphysical?"

"Both."

"I care too much what other people think," I say. He asks what else. "I don't like my calves." He makes a humming noise, taking it in. Then we're both quiet for a while, and he paints.

Here's a weakness I chose not to articulate: I lack restraint. I push things, even when everything is going well. I can't help myself. I know it's unbecoming, but it's as if I have an appetite for something, only I won't know what it is until I hear it. I look at the clock and decide not to say anything for an hour.

"Teach me something about painting," I say two minutes later.

At first, Misha is silent. Then he says: "The tendency is to make the bodies too small. Too small for the heads."

"What's the hardest part?" He doesn't reply, so I ask again. I'm hoping he doesn't say: "The hardest part is getting your subject to shut up."

"The hardest thing is painting the part you find most beautiful."

"What's the most beautiful part about me?" Seems logical enough.

He smiles broadly. "It's all beautiful," he says.

"Come on."

"Your calves."

"Don't be mean. Be serious."

"I'm always serious," he says.

I wonder if he *is* serious. He has the blunt candor of foreigners, and he doesn't censor himself around me, which I like. But there's a lot he doesn't say. I tell my friends he's a riddle wrapped in a mystery inside a blintz. On our first date, I took him to a Persian movie about a boy on a bicycle trying to buy a pair of sneakers for his sister. Afterward, his eyes were bloodshot.

"Did you like it?" I said.

"As a matter of fact, I did."

"You sound surprised."

"I don't like many movies," he said, slipping his ticket stub into his back pocket. "But that was a good one."

The next time we went out, we had drinks with some newlywed friends of his; the previous month, they'd gotten married in Slovenia at a castle whose name sounded like "mock rice." Tiny white lights were twisted through evergreens while we huddled around a heat lamp drinking flavored vodkas. Toward the end of the night I made the mistake of calling myself an open book. Misha burst out laughing and thumped his hand on the table.

"No one who refers to herself as an open book can actually be one," he said.

"But I am," I insisted. His friends were smiling politely. "Whereas you are . . ."

The wife answered for him. "Misha's a closed but readable book," she mused, which at the time I took as a challenge.

On our most recent date, we went dancing. "I'm pretending I wouldn't rather be dead!" I shouted, making fun of the fact that I don't really like to dance, but Misha couldn't understand me over the music. He tilted his head and mouthed, *What?* Later in the evening, this became a private joke between us. I would put my lips next to his ear and whisper what I was going to do to him. He would pretend not to understand, and each time he mouthed *What?* I would lean in and say something steamier, softer.

The next morning, a blinding light flooded his Williamsburg apartment, where we'd slept next to a stack of bare canvases. He commented on the empty bottles of wine in the window seat, complimenting my tolerance.

"We all have our gifts," I said. In truth I felt as if I were wearing an infant-size bike helmet. "Although that last glass might have been gilding the lily." He laughed and suggested "the gilded lily" would be a great name for a cocktail, maybe something with orange juice. A short while later, we set out in search of fried eggs and coffee and a newspaper. But while we ate breakfast, I only pretended to read my section of the paper. Really it was the last thing I was interested in.

"When were you first in love?" I ask. I'm not sure how much time has passed, but the light in the room has frayed, and Misha's water glass is empty.

"That question presumes a couple of things," he says.

"Have you ever been in love?"

His eyes circle the canvas. "Yes," he eventually says. "Once. You?"

"More than once," I say. "Many times."

"Many times?"

"The first time was my sophomore year in college. I adored a junior who lived upstairs from me. I'd climb the steps to his dorm room every night, and we'd talk until the sun came through his circular window. I'd never met anyone so smart. He understood everything. I remember he had this poster of a bullfight on his wall," I say, then cut myself off. I can see from Misha's face that he isn't listening, or rather, he's listening through me, waiting for me to stop. So I do. That bullfight poster had the most vivid colors I've ever seen; the artist must have invented a special pigment to capture the yellow of the sun, the red of the cape. It almost hurt your eyes to look at it, yet you couldn't look away. The junior who lived upstairs from me died of a drug overdose the summer after he graduated. But he taught me one thing I'll never forget: We all desire the cut of truth.

When I stop talking, the room is silent. In another

minute, I'll notice the children's voices down in the street, and the car horns, and the bleating of a delivery truck backing up. But for the moment, everything is still. I watch the illuminated dust particles caught in a nearby shaft of light. They're floating, they're flawless, and in some people, they might produce a feeling of peace. For me, it's just the opposite. I know I should keep quiet, but I can't.

"What's the truest thing you've ever been told?" I say.

At first there's silence. It feels like an unfriendly silence. "The things we're told are never true," Misha says. "The truth must be revealed." He hesitates. "That's our problem here."

I try to keep my forehead from bunching. "What do you mean, 'our problem here'?"

"The difference between you and me."

"I didn't know our difference was a problem."

Misha's weary; he's been working hard; I can see the fatigue in his posture. "Maybe not now," he says, turning away. "But it seems . . . possible. Probable."

"A problem seems probable."

"Yes," he says, and when he turns to me, I can see everything in his face. I feel something behind my rib cage collapse, but I'm careful not to let it show.

"Ask me anything," I say again. I'm sitting with my back straight and my hands folded neatly across my lap. My expression is perfectly neutral; I'm afraid that if I try to smile, I'll cry.

Misha's eyes wake up and his body freezes. "Hold it," he says, putting one hand out as if to stop traffic. His expression has the restrained excitement of a person who has found what he was looking for. "I'm doing your face."

When Misha breaks through, this will be one of his first paintings to sell. It will go to a drawing room on Embassy Row, and my incredulous friends will ask: "Don't you mind sitting naked in front of all those strangers?" But the truth is, I really don't mind being naked. Being naked is the laziest form of revelation.

Misha and I won't break up on this day. He will apologize, excited by his new understanding that the painting is going to turn out well, and he'll hug me, and kiss my hands, and we'll go for crêpes at an old-style Parisian restaurant down the street. But in my mind, this is the day we break up. Things are born in the dark, beneath the soil, in secret.

The actual day we broke up was years ago now, but the thing that has stayed with me most is the irony of that portrait, of having been painted by someone who never really saw me. I complained about this recently to a friend, this disconnect between who we are and how others perceive us. I said: "The trouble is, I'm a fish, but everyone thinks I'm a rabbit." The friend just looked me in the eye and said: "Then why do you surround yourself with people who can only give you carrots?"

The dust particles continue to dance in their column of light. The cushion has finally stopped itching me, and the Hasidic grocery is closing up shop. I'm not sure what I'm thinking about—the Persian movie or that bullfight poster or my grandmother's hair catching fire—when it finally registers that Misha is speaking to me.

"Ruby," he's saying. He pulls me to my feet. He's

hugging me, happy. "Ruby." He takes my hands, and I look into his face, momentarily confused, trying to shake the feeling that I'm gazing into the face of a stranger. "It is finished," he says, and we both take a step back, to better see what we have made.

# THE SUMMER BEFORE

This was the summer before the divorce. I was thirteen, and Sarah was twelve; Lindsay had just turned six. Sarah and I spent our time looking for excuses to get away from our two-bedroom cottage, with its sullen moods and sudden thunder. Lindsay followed wherever we went. She'd started sucking her thumb again that year, and insisted on wearing the same bathing suit, the one covered in floppy purple tulips, every single day.

We trusted the lake, but we didn't trust Lindsay. She eavesdropped constantly and had the spooky habit of showing up in our plans before we even knew what they were. One morning, while our mom and dad were arguing about the nature of "facts" while bacon popped and splattered on the stove, we got a call from the Zimmerman brothers, asking us to meet them at the rope swing. Sarah and I slipped away quietly, but when we got down to the dock, there was Lindsay, already seated in the *Lightning Bug,* our small yellow outboard.

"Get out of the boat, Lindsay," I said. "Now."

She kept her eyes lowered and didn't move; she didn't even dare suck her thumb. I leaned on the side of the boat with my foot, tilting it down. Water rushed in, and Lindsay gasped, but she stayed put.

"Stand up!" I said. I yanked my foot away and the boat lurched. Lindsay braced herself and looked up. When our eyes met, her lower lip began to quiver.

"Mom says that if you go in the boat, you have to take me with you," she said.

"Mom's not here," I said. "And you're not coming."

"Come on, Lindz, just get out," Sarah said, glancing back at the house.

I tried a softer tone. "We don't have time for this today," I said. "You can come with us next time."

"That's what you said last time!" she said. "You promised!" Quick tears slipped in straight lines down her cheeks. Sarah and I exchanged a look. It was clear she wasn't going to leave without a scene, and if we didn't get out of there soon, no one would be going anywhere.

"You can't ride in the boat without a life jacket," I said with an exaggerated sigh. *Mom says.* I folded my arms. "Go on, get one. And hurry up."

Lindsay leaped up and made a sprint for the porch, her small feet thudding gleefully against the dock's wooden planks. And while she scurried, we scurried, too.

"Wait!" she cried, returning just in time to see Sarah pulling in the bumpers as I steered the boat away. "Come back—please—wait for me!" She poked her head through her life preserver and frantically clipped its buckles, demonstrating her readiness. Then she stood on the end of the dock and waited, long after it should have been obvious we weren't coming back. Sarah took the seat beside me, I hit the throttle, and neither one of us turned around. But in my mind's eye, as we sped away, I could still see her standing there: just a tiny blond head atop a bright orange puff.

At night, it only got worse. Dad bought us a tent that summer and set it up on the pine needles between our cottage and the lake so we could sleep in our own front yard but feel as if we were camping. We loved that tent— a Coleman Deluxe All-Weather Two-Man. But with Lindsay, it was three. Sarah and I did our best to ignore her as we discussed the important innovations Zack and James Zimmerman had been introducing us to. Most recently, it was spin the bottle.

"Are you supposed to stay for more than a minute?" Sarah said.

"Only stay for as long as you feel like," I said. "Personally, I wouldn't give James more than two seconds. One, two—you're out!" I sliced the air with my hand, and we both laughed. Zack and James were fraternal twins, fourteen, and handsome. They were handsome, we'd decided, not cute. They tanned faster than we did, skipped rocks farther, and water-skied better—they could slalom, and jump the wake. Once they bought us candy necklaces at the Old Country Store and then tried to bite off the candy while they were around our necks.

I crawled forward so our foreheads were almost touching. "Zack stuck his tongue in my mouth," I said.

"He *did*?" I couldn't tell if she was delighted or repulsed. I nodded gravely. When it happened, I wasn't sure if I was delighted or repulsed myself. But in retrospect, I'd decided I liked it. It seemed the mature thing to do. Besides, I liked Zack, sort of. I mean, it was strange that he and James were twins; they were so different. Zack was the more attractive one, with bold hazel eyes and long, elegant fingers. His mother loved to tell the story of how when he was born, the obstetrician had said: "This boy has the hands of a surgeon or a pianist." And his father had added: "Or a pickpocket."

James, with pale auburn curls, was the sweet one. "Are you sure you want to?" he'd asked both Sarah and me before we started. Zack had gone looking for an empty bottle on the other side of the island, where older teenagers made campfires. "We can always go for a boat ride, or do something else." He spoke in a low voice, as if afraid Zack might hear him.

"We're sure," I said quickly, worried that any hesitation would make us look bad.

"Well, just remember," he said, but then he stopped.

"What?" His expression was so contorted, I laughed.

"Nothing," he said. He started to walk away. "Meg," he began, turning around, but before he could get to the rest Zack came bounding out of the woods, brandishing an empty glass bottle with curvy white lettering.

"Got it!" he said. Then he winked and handed the bottle to me.

Sarah still couldn't believe the part about the tongue.

"Did you . . . like it?" she asked. Her gaze passed back and forth between my eyes and my mouth, as if my lips could answer for me. I cracked a smile, and we both burst out laughing.

"What do kisses taste like?" Lindsay's voice from the corner of the tent came as a surprise. She'd been so quiet, we'd almost forgotten she was there.

"This doesn't concern you, Thumb," I said. I swung the flashlight toward her. "And don't you dare say one word to Mom."

Of course, camping was only a camouflage. As soon as Lindsay fell asleep, Sarah and I bypassed the noisy zippers and pulled ourselves out of our sleeping bags like snakes shedding skins. We hurried along the dirt road, crickets chirping and a full moon overhead. The Zimmermans lived ten houses away, and Zack and James had arranged to sleep out in their boathouse. I pinged my finger against the screen. James materialized first.

"Sorry we're late," I said.

"No worries," he said. "It's not like we had somewhere else to be." Behind him, Zack was putting something in a cooler. We heard a loud noise that sounded as if it came from the house, and everybody froze. Zack put his finger to his lips, and I rolled my eyes—as if we didn't know. We remained motionless for another few seconds, then Zack brushed past, tapping my elbow.

"Now or never," he said.

The Zimmermans had a white and silver Sea Ray with cushioned seats and a chrome steering wheel. It was a sleek boat, perfect for water-skiing behind during the day. But tonight we had something else in mind. Zack knelt in the bow and paddled us away from the dock—we didn't dare start the motor this close to the house—while James spread out a blanket so the rest of us could lie down. Once we'd reached a safe distance, Zack turned the ignition key, and we began speeding through the dark water.

James took off his sweatshirt and handed it to me. "Your lips are turning blue," he said. Sarah and I hadn't thought to wear more than cotton shorts and T-shirts. I was so grateful that in my happiness I shared it with Sarah, draping it across both our legs.

When we reached the middle of the bay, Zack cut the motor and let the boat ghost across the lake's glassy surface. Everything was still; only a few loons wailed in the distance. It sounded as if they were mother loons calling for their children, and I began to think about my mom. About how lately she'd cry at nothing, and how she seemed anxious all the time. In my dreams she was tiny, small enough to fit in the palm of my hand, and I would cup my fingers around her and rescue her from stampeding herds and fiery buildings.

The boat swayed as small waves lapped at its sides. James put a cassette in the tape deck, and a ballad by Journey started to play. Zack tossed back another blanket he found in the bow, where he was rummaging around with the cooler. Sarah, James, and I lay under the blanket and stared up at the sky. The black silhouettes of pine trees put a jagged frame around its glittering endlessness. My uncle had been teaching me about photography, and I wondered if it would ever be possible to do justice to this simple sight. Something about the water all around and the sky all above gave me a real sense of being on the planet.

"We're on planet Earth," I said.

Zack let out a long whistle from the bow. "Are you high?" asked his disembodied voice.

James turned to me. "There are so many stars, but at the same time, it's all so . . . precise. You know? As if each star is necessary. As if everything happens the way it's supposed to happen," he said.

*That's not true,* I thought. *My mother isn't supposed to be so unhappy, and everything isn't meant to be so broken.* I kept quiet, though, because I wanted him to say more. But James was silent. Then I remembered his other silence, the one on the island, and I was about to ask him what he was going to tell me that day, before Zack came bounding out of the woods, but I couldn't, I couldn't ask him anything, because a second later the silhouette of his head blocked the stars, and I could feel him breathe, and then he kissed me—a real kiss. It wasn't like spin the bottle at all. It was different—sad or something. Sad but great.

After he lay back down I turned to him, but he kept his eyes pinned to the sky. He reached over and took my hand. To this day, I can't explain what made that night seem so magical, or why I felt such a stab of affection when James Zimmerman took my hand. Maybe if I could, I'd be able to explain why on the way home, once Sarah and I were alone on the dirt road, I began to cry. I wept softly, wiping my nose with the sleeve of his sweatshirt.

"Everything's going to be okay," Sarah said, which

only made me cry more. We walked the rest of the way without speaking. When we got back to the tent, Lindsay was gone.

We ran into the house, checked the bunk beds, the bathroom, the kitchen, the porch. Panic rose in our throats. It was 2:30 A.M. I hovered outside the door to our parents' bedroom, feeling sick to my stomach, finally nerving myself to go in.

"Mom," I said, rocking her shoulder. "Wake up. We can't find Lindsay."

She didn't understand at first, but once she did, she didn't linger long enough to get mad. Immediately she began searching through rooms, halting in doorways, flipping on lights. When had we last seen her? How had this happened? She called our father's name, and he appeared.

"Lindsay's gone missing," she said.

"What? How?"

She ignored him. While she looked under the beds, I told Dad what had happened. Then she headed outside.

"Elizabeth. Wait," he said. He grabbed her arm, but she yanked it away. He turned to me. "Call the Beckers; ask if they've seen her." But I couldn't move. My limbs were lead; my mind was stupefied. Instead, I watched as my mother headed into the lake.

This was the shape of my mother's courage: a zigzag path, cut through deeper and deeper water, as she walked in lines parallel with the shore, waiting for the blunt feel of flesh that would be the body of her youngest child. I stood in the doorway and stared; there was nothing I could do. Sarah was in the woods behind the house, calling Lindsay's name—now a hollow, ghostly sound. Dad was on the dirt road in his slippers, shining a flashlight into the trees.

Two hours passed. Or maybe it was twenty minutes. Mrs. Becker had appeared and was standing on the beach, hugging her ribs. "Liz, be careful," she kept saying. The water was up to my mother's collarbones. Mrs. Becker took me aside. "Go inside and call the police," she said, adding: "What in the name of God were you girls thinking?"

I couldn't breathe. What would I possibly say to the police? "I did it, officer. I lost her, I drowned her, I hit her with a car. And all she ever wanted—" Wait a minute.

"Mom!" I said, running for the dock, dizzy from the sudden rush of hope. I got to the boat, pulled back the tarp, and there, asleep, with her thumb in her mouth, was Lindsay—*alive*—with her life jacket on. "I found her," I tried to say, but the words caught in my throat, came spilling out my eyes. *Mom. Come here. I found her.*

Today, Lindsay is sunbathing on a chaise longue that's older than she is. Its plastic mesh is faded and fraying like straw. It's late August, and she's wearing a brand-new bikini whose borders don't quite reach the high-tide mark left by its predecessor. One tanned leg is extended the length of the chaise; the other is bent at the knee. Her hair, a deep honey blond now, is piled on top of her head, and she's wearing those oversize sunglasses, the kind movie stars wear. Lindsay is seventeen.

I went away for a few years, packed all my belongings in a duffel bag, sneaked out in the middle of the night, the whole deal. But now I'm back, and Lindsay and I are trying to get along. Everyone acts as if I've changed, but I haven't. Or rather: We've all changed. That summer was my first taste of wanting something more, of believing there was something out in the world for me. So I did it. I made my escape. I wasn't trying to hurt anyone else; I was only trying to save myself. Still, when I returned— out of money and out of options—Lindsay acted as if I had abandoned her personally.

My eyes are on the low range of mountains across the lake. Lindsay's head is tilted toward the sun. She makes the *come here* gesture with her hand.

"Give it to me," she says.

*"Pusillanimous."*

"Oh, man," she sighs. The *P*'s are her weak spot. "Give me a hint."

"When your animus needs a poos."

She bolts upright. "Is this another one of your sex words?" she laughs. "'Cause I don't know what the SAT was like back in your day. But it's rated G now." She pats my shoulder. "I'm going to go make a sandwich. Want anything?"

"No, thanks," I say, and she walks away, the balls of her feet leaving swirled pivots in the sand.

While she's gone, I stare at the old house. It looks deserted. The wood is gray-black, and in many places, it's falling apart. After the divorce, Mom always said there wasn't enough money to fix anything, but it seemed as if there was more to it than that. During the school year, when he's not giving lectures or presenting papers at a foreign university, we still see Dad every other Sunday, and he's still his same quiet, bespectacled self. But this place feels like an abandoned set where we once filmed some scenes, an artifact from some other life, made even stranger by its eerie familiarity.

Sarah is studying in Barcelona for the summer, drinking sangria and mastering the language. In her postcards, her handwriting has become curvier. "Barcelona is an extremely humid city," she writes. "The pickpocket capital of the world."

I twist my finger around a thread at the bottom of my cut-off shorts and snap it off. I'm wearing sunblock, plus a baseball cap. Lindsay is the only one in our family who tans. Sometimes, when I'm on an outdoor shoot, I'll slather on so much SPF 45 that the other assistants tease me. "Step aside, Meg, you're a secondary source of light." Or: "Watch out, she'll cast a shadow." Especially Ed—he likes to rib me the most. "You glow," he says. I refuse to go out with him. Mostly I ignore them all and try to focus on adjusting the backdrop and prepping the subject. I have to admit, I like what I do. There's something about being on the hidden side of the camera that suits me.

I hear the screen door slap, and Lindsay walks over with a BLT on a paper plate. The smell of bacon takes me by surprise.

"You know," she says, settling back into her chair, "Winnipesaukee means 'Smile of the Great Spirit.'" Her sandwich is cut in half, and she hands one piece to me.

"I know," I say, giving it back to her. "But that won't be on your test." She bites off a corner, rests the plate on her stomach, stretches out, and chews.

"*Perspicacious,*" I say, a few minutes later. Lindsay sits up and grins.

"I know that one," she says. "That means you have to come sailing with me."

"No, it doesn't," I say. "I thought you were serious about getting these down." I don't particularly care whether Lindsay studies or not; I just don't feel like getting up.

But she's already fetching the Sunfish from the side of the house. "I need a break," she says. "*You* need a break. Besides, it'll be fun. I can give you another lesson. Remember how you almost capsized us?"

"No," I say. "I don't."

She drags the boat down to the lake and stands at the water's edge, waiting for me. "This may be our last chance. Who knows if I'll even come back here after I go off to college."

"Oh, I'm sorry. I thought you *wanted* to do better on the SAT. Last I checked, there was no guarantee you were even going to get into any colleges."

Her face goes blank. Then she drops the boat and heads for the house.

"Lindz, listen—"

"No, you listen," she says, stopping in her tracks. "Why do you always say no to everything? Why do you pretend you don't want anything, when we can all see how much you really do?"

"What are you even talking about?"

"What do you think I'm talking about? Your *life.*"

"See, that's the part you don't get," I say, laughing a little. "I really *don't* want anything."

"It's so transparent, it's pathetic."

"And I certainly don't want anything from you," I say, not laughing anymore. "You don't know the first thing about me, so let's both stop pretending you do. Go on, go sailing. Waste your life."

Lindsay starts toward the house again, but then, in a single, fluid motion, she spins around, goes back to the water, gets in the boat, and sails.

I don't watch her. Instead I turn to the neighbors' house, the Beckers, and I remember the summer we lost her. That was the last summer James and Zack's family rented a cottage here; they bought a ski place in Vermont the following year and started going there for summers as well. But our mothers kept in touch, and Mom told me their father sent Zack away to military school when things got really bad, so now they're waiting to see if he makes it home in one piece. I guess active duty is still part of the military school bargain. It's hard to imagine Zack in combat, though; beneath all the bravado, there was such quiet fear.

And James, James who kissed me, apparently James fell in love while at college in the Midwest—Fran was her name, I think—and became engaged just after graduation. But six months later, in the middle of planning their wedding, one day Fran had trouble stepping off a curb. After a bunch of tests, they discovered she had Lou Gehrig's disease. She wanted to call off the wedding, but James insisted. So they got married, and a month before their first anniversary, with James by her side, she died. Fran died, and James became a twenty-three-year-old widower. Sometimes I can't help but wonder, if I were ever to see him again, if there would be a way to ask him, without hurting him: *Does* everything happen the way it's supposed to, James? Do you still think so? This rotting house, my half-alive mother, your wife, my sister? My sister, who every time I look at her, I remember what she said when I first came back: "You left without saying good-bye."

I turn to the lake just as the broad red and yellow stripes catch the bright wind. Lindsay's is the only boat out there, and it's perfect. I lied before, about "Smile of the Great Spirit." I've been coming to this lake for nearly twenty years, and I never knew what the name meant. Where does she learn these things? Who ever taught her? I don't remember ever teaching her a single thing. All the while, hidden in the background, she must have listened and learned in the echoes and silences the rest of us didn't even know we made.

But she's not in the background anymore. That's what's changed; that's the difference between my sister and me. She's on the other side of the camera. And so unafraid. I watch the boat and, in spite of myself, I'm proud of her. Against the orange sun, her sail looks like wings.

I go to the end of the dock, sit down, and wait. *Come home,* I think, staring at the bright sail. *Come back.* The words are disorienting, and for a second I don't know who I'm talking to. I pull my legs against my chest and begin to rock back and forth. *Come back, come back,* my body is saying, until I'm not even looking at the boat anymore, but my eyes are pressed against my knees, and I realize I've begun to cry.

# MOLLUSK MAKES

## A COMEBACK

In her twenties, Katie was struggling to find a beautiful path. Having discovered what was false, she was waiting to encounter what was true. But thus far, the quest for something changeless and good had left her penniless and depressed. Every day she would eye the homeless man who hung around her block with a growing sense of kinship. She liked his signs. WE'RE ALL IN THIS TOGETHER, or WE ALL NEED A LITTLE HELP SOMETIMES. Once he'd even had the wisdom to write WE GROW RICH ONLY THROUGH WHAT WE GIVE, which Katie felt should surely be the universal slogan of all panhandlers.

She'd lost two jobs in two weeks. First, a businessman had come into the Barnes & Noble near Lincoln Center where she was stacking the shelves and working the registers. As she totaled his pile of CliffsNotes, she'd said gently: "I realize these are convenient—God knows I've used them myself plenty of times—but you might go back and read the books sometime. Maybe later, or in addition, or something."

The slick head thought about this. "Yeah, I could do that," he said. Then, casually handing her a hundred-dollar bill, he'd added: "But then again, look where that got you." She didn't know what he must have said to her manager, but the next day, without warning, she was fired.

The following week she went to work in a midtown office besieged by phone calls. On her first morning, she'd had to say: "Thanks for holding, can I help you?" so many times in a row that she'd once said: "Thanks for helping, can I hold you?" An honest mistake, but apparently one that was not much appreciated by the client. Then, at the end of the day, she and her supervisor had entered the elevator together. As she pushed the button for the lobby, she'd said to him: "I assume we're both going to L," which came out sounding like something that was not at all what she meant. She wasn't exactly surprised when, at the end of the week, she wasn't asked back.

Now she'd reached the stage where she was having difficulty mustering even enough energy to do laundry or open mail. Her friends weren't any help. She tried explaining her malaise to her best friend, Emily, but Emily's boyfriend, Roy, cut in.

"The point of life," he said, "as I thought I'd taught you by now, is to try to suck as much pleasure out of each passing moment as you possibly can." But Katie was convinced there had to be more to life than pleasure-sucking. Besides, she wasn't about to take the advice of Roy, someone whose life ambition was to have a furniture store called The Sofa King, just so he could run ads that said: "Our prices are So-fa-King low."

Emily was more understanding. "Something good's going to come your way, I just know it," she said. "All you need is for one little thing to go right, and everything else could fall into place from there."

Katie was doubtful. She looked everywhere, even though she didn't know what she was looking for. She was becoming an insomniac, so she found herself watching a lot of late-night TV. Plenty of people were doling out advice; it's just that no one ever said anything useful. She clicked through infomercials selling things everybody knew nobody needed, and an old movie whose emotional climax she'd just missed. "What are you running from?" Clark Gable asked as he clutched the trench-coated arm of a perfectly coiffed blonde. "What is it you're so afraid of?" Most disheartening were the reruns of a daytime talk-show host who seemed to think that tough love was the answer to everything. Diabetes? Tough love! This was what her species had to show for itself?

She went to the Museum of Natural History, figuring if she couldn't find a sense of connectedness among her own kind, maybe seeing the full wingspan of life would console her somehow. But it was no use. Like everything else, the museum left her with more questions than answers. The mollusks in particular irritated her. What was so great about shellfish that they deserved their own wing?

Even the dodo bird, *Raphus cucullatus* as he was formally called, was a mystery. It was speculated he had become complacent because of a lack of predators. In the absence of enemies, he grew unwary, got fat, and forgot how to fly. His ancestors must have known how to fly, the little metal plaque said, in order to reach the small island of Mauritius in the middle of the Indian Ocean, where Dodo lived. But Dodo himself was just a flightless pigeon. He became extinct around 1700, killed by, among other things, semiwild pigs liberated by the Europeans. His original Latin name, from Linnaeus, was *Didus ineptus*— an appellation given post-extinction, in what Katie concluded was perhaps the greatest ever example of adding insult to injury.

She looked at Ineptus tenderly, wanting to touch him, but he was in his Plexiglas case. "What is it you're running from?" she whispered, aware of the competent strangers all around her. "What are you so afraid of?" Lately she would lie awake for hours, wondering whether she should look for a place with cheaper rent? Move to a cheaper city? Apply to graduate school? Learn how to waitress? Maybe she should have studied French wines in college instead of French literature. She shielded her face with the collar of her Windbreaker so the young mothers juggling strollers and BlackBerrys wouldn't hear her addressing the bird. "Tell me what to do," she said.

Things continued to deteriorate. The fact that she had recently fallen into the habit of masturbating to thoughts of George Gordon, the sixth Lord Byron, was not a good sign. Although generally speaking, she was an advocate of masturbation. "Sleep with a person, and you please him for a night. Teach him to masturbate, and you please him for a lifetime," she would occasionally joke to her closest friends. Katie was not ashamed of Lord

Byron. You had to be resourceful in life; she'd learned that early on. Now even her resourcefulness was coming to an end.

One snowy afternoon in early February, she ducked into Fliks Video, hoping for a miracle. Emily had once given her a quote that Katie liked so much, she carried it around on a scrap of paper in her wallet. *A miracle is nothing more than justice postponed, arriving to compensate those it had cruelly abandoned.*

"I'm looking for a movie where justice is served," she said to the greasy-haired teenager behind the counter.

He stared at her blankly. "You mean, like, Schwarzenegger?"

"Not exactly," Katie sighed. "It's all right. I'll look for myself." But as she ambled along, scanning the shelves, nothing promised to be the hope-giving, wisdom-packed wallop she was searching for. Only then, as she stared at the rows of box covers, at the pictures of people laughing or embracing or crying, all caught in the heroic struggles of their lives, did a small thought occur to her with such simplicity she almost said it aloud: *I am afraid to try.*

Emily and Roy attempted to cheer her up. They cooked her Middle Eastern food, poured her wine. "You're talented! You're gorgeous!" they said. "Tell it to my landlord," said Katie. She stared at her couscous, not eating. Couscous always reminded her of cooked sand—that was probably its proper translation. Where did people muster the energy to harvest the desert and cook it? Where did everyone find the will to do all the work in the world? We're all allowed a kind of grace period, she decided, when we can coast along, before we really need to choose a life and summon the determination to live it. Her grace period had just run out.

The following Tuesday, Valentine's Day, her phone was disconnected and her car was towed. Katie tried to remain cheerful in the face of disaster. *Well, at least I'm not Ineptus,* she thought. Maybe that would be her slogan for the day. She practiced saying: "Look, I am not Ineptus," and "This is not an Ineptus you're dealing with here, folks."

On top of that, it was cold cold cold. It was one of those days she wished her blow-dryer were battery-operated so she could stick it in her pants before she left the apartment.

She went to the municipal building where you pay penalties and back-tickets. It quickly became clear that her strategy of avoidance had not been the best way to deal with parking violations. To get her car back would cost four more dollars than she had in her checking account. She asked the stout, thin-lipped woman behind the counter if she could borrow four dollars.

"No," the woman said.

Her eyes came to rest on the string of tissue-paper hearts hanging above the woman's head. "Where's the love?" said Katie. The woman did not smile. The people in line behind her grumbled. Then she remembered her emergency cash. She opened her wallet and unfolded a weather-beaten five-dollar bill. Emily had always teased her about it anyway. "Yeah, that'll get you out of any emergency whose solution is a chai latte," she said. After her account was settled, the woman gave her a slip of paper on which was written the address of the tow lot:

770 Zerega Avenue, the Unlimited Tow Company, the Bronx.

Next she went to the Verizon payment center at Second Avenue and Thirteenth Street, just around the corner from her apartment. She waited in a long line; it seemed it was a busy time of year for the phone-disconnecting business. In general, it was not a very happy place. As if it weren't bad enough that they disconnected your phone, they made you hang around with the kind of people who got their phones disconnected. She imagined a TV camera rolling into the room. People in rollers and sweatpants would still smile ghoulishly and wave. "Hi, Mom!" *Hi! I'm here getting my phone reconnected because I'm pretty much a failure, but Hi!*

She wrote the phone company a bad check. Just a small fiction that, like most fiction, had a strong foundation in truth. The money had been in her checking account just that morning, before she had to bail her car out of jail. She felt terrible handing it over to the nice man behind the counter, all smiles, but what else was she supposed to do? She'd once had to write a bad check to the post office at Christmastime, when she was mailing her packages home. And they'd been very understanding when she sent them the money a month later, saying they wouldn't send the federal agents after all. It appeared that in her efforts to get some fuzzy mittens to her sister, Katie had committed a felony.

Walking away from the counter, she remembered that she still had a small amount of money left in her savings account. She'd always liked the idea of savings, even if she wasn't particularly keen on its practice. She liked calling it saving, too, because it was like that: You think you're saving something, when actually, it saves you.

But she needed to transfer the money right away, before the phone company discovered her check was bad. It was after five o'clock, but there was still telebanking. Perhaps there was a use, after all, for the rampant inbreeding of technology and information, and all their mutant offspring.

She used the pay phone across the street from her apartment. It must have been the coldest day in the history of winter. Too bad she couldn't go inside and use her own phone, but she understood that sometimes it's hard to fix a thing by using the thing that needs fixing.

She put in a quarter and did a little jump-dance to try to get warm. For such-and-such corporate account, press 3; for such-and-such-and-such credit card, press 7. She plumbed the depths of her purse for more change and came up with a few nickels. Several yards away, the homeless man was sitting on a piece of cardboard, feeding pigeons out of a grimy paper bag. How could anyone be whistling on a day like this? One of the birds wandered over to Katie. She ignored it, but it wouldn't go away.

"I don't have anything for you," she said. "I've got my own problems here." The bird cooed softly in the snow at her feet.

She pressed more buttons and waited. Not only were they making her jump through countless audio hoops, but the worst part was, every time she got within sight of her goal she was mysteriously disconnected. It seemed that modern technology was not the perfect überland all the ads claimed it would be.

She was almost out of change when she was disconnected, again. She was incredulous. She was beside herself. But she wouldn't give up. She couldn't give up. She had to at least be able to do this one little thing.

She started over. Numbers, shivering, coins.

*Click.*

She stared at the pigeon, wanted to wring its feathery little purple-gray neck. "I am not a Dodo bird!" she shouted. "Go away!"

The homeless man looked up when she yelled. He gazed at her, and for the first time, she noticed his sign.

YOU'RE JUST ABOUT TO GET TO THE GOOD PART, it read.

Had she begun to hallucinate? Her vision was blurry; she blinked and stared. Then she walked over to him.

"Is that for me?" she said. "Did you write that for me?" The homeless man just smiled, a toothless, beatific smile, and rattled his paper cup. Katie dropped in her last quarter.

She walked all the way to the Bronx. The snow was stiff and crusty, but she was wearing sturdy boots, and was able to make steady progress. The air seemed to have gotten warmer, too. She was not a Dodo bird, complacent unto extinction. She was a mollusk, barnacled and determined. She would survive. She would survive and multiply, until one day entire wings of museums would be filled with her kind. *Mollusk makes a comeback,* she thought. Her cheeks were pink from the cold, which her mother always said brought out her good looks, and her lips were rosy with her new favorite lipstick. It was officially called "Brick," but Katie had conceived of a better name: "I'm not really a waitress."

She marched to the Unlimited Tow Company, and on the way, she made a plan. On the cross streets, she asked her feet questions: "What are you so afraid of? What is it you're running from?" And on the avenues, she made them reply: "We're afraid of failure, and afraid of success. We are afraid of being loved, and afraid of being alone. The world is full of pain, and this is scary. And the world is crazy-beautiful, and that's daunting, too. Worst of all, so little is under our control." When she heard this last answer, she stopped and struck a deal. "All you have to do is try," she said. "Okay?" Her feet resumed their motion. That was their way of nodding.

She would eventually get to the tow lot and pass through a chain-link fence into the sea of automobiles. Somewhere there would be a man in a heated trailer who would take her receipt and show her to her car. Somewhere there would be a good part, waiting to begin.

# I KNEW YOU'D

## BE LOVELY

His birthday was only three days away, and Hannah had to find Tom the perfect gift: prescient, ingenious, unique, unforgettable. All month she'd been looking for clues from the universe. She scoured the Internet, studied mail-order catalogs, stole peeks inside other people's briefcases. Finally she found herself resorting to desperate measures, and was trying to read the minds of the men seated across from her on the commuter train. She stared at them under the bright lights and asked telepathically: *What do you want most in the whole world that costs under two hundred dollars and would fit in a box?*

Her psychic acumen, however, was proving to be as dim as her prospects. To make matters worse, she'd been caught squinting purposefully at strangers, a posture she quickly tried to pass off as an attempt to read the contact-lens advertisements. By the time she got to work, she had the kind of headache that made her think she might in fact *need* contact lenses. She was also on the verge of full-scale panic. Hannah knew that if she didn't find the gift that demonstrated she, better than anyone, understood the very contours of Tom's soul, she could lose him.

There was another woman. Tom had done everything he could to assure Hannah the woman was just a pen pal, and described what they had as that clever little word, a *correspondence*. But it was easy for Hannah to tell that her nemesis was no mere pal of the pen. She was more like a *Playboy* centerfold with stationery.

Tom met the woman six months ago, at a summer writing seminar in Prague. Hannah's first warning sign came when she was relating the story to her best friend.

"He met her at some summer camp? What'd they do, sit around, toast marshmallows, and sing by the campfire?"

"It wasn't a summer camp. It was a writing workshop."

"*Oh,*" Nihan said, shaking out her cigarette match. "So they sat around, drank whiskey, and screwed."

As it happened, when Tom returned to Boston in September, he *was* somewhat aglow, but Hannah assumed that had something to do with renewed confidence and nutritious Czech food. True, he proceeded to commit to his work with inordinate enthusiasm—retreating from Hannah a bit in the process—but this seemed the natural consequence of a summer of encouragement. In fact, she thought she'd read something about that in the brochure. The brochure that had featured all kinds of attractive young writers, huddled in clusters of smiling excitement.

Back in college, when Tom was first courting her, Hannah used to tease him about his wavy brown locks and gold-rimmed spectacles.

"You're too good-looking to be a poet." Five years later she'd learned better than to encourage him along those lines. But she did encourage his writing. So although he seemed distant, Hannah stood by her belief in the need for solitude and selfishness—of the good kind—when it came to one's work. Nihan rolled her eyes.

"True intimacy embraces a certain distance," Hannah said.

"Sure," Nihan chuckled. "Whatever."

But Hannah let Tom have his space and tried not to feel threatened. She reasoned that she would have every advantage over an opponent: She *knew* Tom, knew his weakness for World War II documentaries, knew his secret dream of becoming a competitive Scrabble champion, knew he often laughed in his sleep. She understood that he considered himself to be "Capricorn, nonpracticing," and that he'd once set out to read the dictionary but had only gotten as far as *D*. When he was depressed he liked to go to the movies by himself, and when his back was giving him trouble, it sometimes helped if she walked on it for him. This nefarious newcomer would be no match for her—why, she *lived* with Tom (had the home-court advantage), and his would-be seductress didn't even live in the same state.

But as soon as the leaves began to turn, her letters started to arrive. No, they couldn't use e-mail like the rest of the world. Apparently the girl either had some quaint notion about the benefits of real paper and real penmanship or she was simply too dumb to know how to connect to a server. Before long, Hannah found herself resenting the postman and rethinking his holiday bonus of baked goods. And she would cringe at the heavy, eggshell-colored envelopes addressed with slanted loops of red ink—the felt-tipped marker of Satan's minion, to be sure.

Hannah and Tom had a happy relationship built on five years of commitment and trust—qualities that were beginning to feel like small, cold pebbles compared with the heated rush of novelty. So when the New York post-mark began showing up more and more frequently—sometimes twice in one week—Hannah started asking questions.

"What does she look like, anyway?" she said one Saturday in October as she placed a stack of mail on the kitchen table. Tom glanced up from the paper just as the kettle began to hiss.

"Who?" he said, predictably.

"Girl." He and Hannah both knew who "girl" referred to; no use feigning ignorance. He turned a page and refolded the paper.

"Well, she's blond," he said.

"Oh, she's *blond*, is she?" Hannah said, as if *blond* were the Czech word for "fellatio addict." Hannah was strawberry blond herself, with a dusting of freckles across her nose. "That figures," she muttered. "Go on," she said. "Continue."

"And she's, well, I'd say she's about your height." Five feet six inches of Hannah was standing in front of his chair. Tom scanned from her ankles to her eyebrows. "Yeah. Your height," he said. "If I had to guess."

Evidently, she was going to have to help him along.

"And breasts?" she said, crossing her arms.

"Yes. She has breasts."

"I knew it! So just what are these breasts of hers like?" Hannah's breasts were a little on the small side, although perfectly shaped, well-rounded with pretty pink nipples.

"I wouldn't know," Tom said. "I slept through the class where everyone came topless."

Hannah stepped up and straddled his chair. "Don't try to tell me you haven't imagined what they're like, mister," she said. She wagged her finger at him, in order to be herself and make fun of herself at the same time. "Even *I've* imagined what they're like by now." Tom snapped at her finger with his teeth. "I mean it," she said. "Don't make me hurt you."

"Please, hurt me!" he said. He pulled her into his lap. "Give the man a break," he said. "He doesn't know what he's doing. He isn't all that sharp." He kissed her temple. "Besides, you know he'd pull the moon for you." He imagined Hannah knew full well he *would*, too. He also imagined Sydney's breasts were magnificent: smooth and luscious.

Although Tom was somewhat charmed by Hannah's unprecedented antics at first, before long he was curious to know what kind of justice could exist in a world that would allow him to be punished for sex he didn't even have. He was smart enough not to want points for resisting temptation, because he knew the need for resistance betrayed the presence of temptation, which for most women was as much a sin as mattress-gripping, pore-cleansing sex that lifted the bedposts and rattled the fishbowl. But then again, Hannah wasn't like most women.

The two met their senior year in college while she was working at the student union. Tom loved to watch her, her hair twisted up, dewy and serious as she steamed milk for other undergrads' cappuccinos. It didn't take long for him to develop a serious caffeine habit. Soon they were an item.

They would go to the library together and stack their books by the big window in the quiet section. Tom knew the sign-language alphabet and liked to think he could invent intuitive hand signals for anything he didn't have time to spell out. But every gesture he invented looked a lot like the hula wave, and he would only make Hannah crack up, and then they'd be asked to leave.

Hannah knew Tom would dump his pen pal if she asked him to, which was part of the reason she would never ask. She wasn't the kind of person to issue mandates or start sentences with phrases like, "If you loved me." She wasn't even sure how other women pulled that off. If you loved me, you wouldn't . . . write letters? Or, no letters to women? No letters to attractive women? Ah, yes: "You wouldn't do something you knew upset me." But the thing that was upsetting was that in her mind, it was Tom's choice. It wasn't that she wanted to take all the spice out of his life. It was just that, as the conspicuous correspondence grew and grew, she couldn't help feeling left out.

One night in mid-December, while they were having dinner at their favorite Thai restaurant and deciding what to do afterward, Hannah suggested they rent a skin flick just as the chicken with peanut sauce was arriving. Before Tom could answer, she started to cry. That was when he realized he was going to have to do something. When they got home that night, he handed over the stack of letters.

Hannah took them into the bedroom and closed the door. For the next two hours she roamed through the childhood embarrassments, coffee-shop epiphanies, and myriad curiosities of a woman named Sydney. The young writer's life seemed to consist mainly of repeated encounters with ridiculous situations wherein she was lacking adequate monies, workable transportation, appropriate clothing, or some absurd combination of all three. Apparently she had grown up in Boston and still had family in the area.

As Hannah had anticipated, flirtation and innuendo were there, sneering at her all over the place. But in truth there was nothing that betrayed any untoward activities. At one point, Sydney even referred to something Tom had written about Hannah as "candid and tender." There was, however, one passage that struck her as alarming:

> I must have been born defective, without the jealousy gene, because I never feel the possessive kind of love. Today I was at the museum, looking at one of those really beautiful nature paintings, where the loneliness seems almost holy. I felt a kind of solidarity with the other people who were admiring it alongside me. Then I imagined someone in the group running up and shielding it with his arms, how ridiculous that would be. Yet how common it is to encounter the feeling, "I love you because you're mine." It stuns me, all the things we're willing to forsake for security, which is only ever imaginary anyway.

Hannah emerged from the bedroom. She wanted to reward what she knew had been a magnanimous gesture by keeping her questions to a minimum.

Tom put his book facedown in his lap. "Still want to rent a skin flick?" he said.

She handed him the stack of letters, this one on top. "What are your thoughts on all this?"

"Isn't it plain? I told you not to worry. She doesn't even want a boyfriend. She talks of nothing but liberty. In fact, I get the feeling she might pitch for both teams."

"Oh, *really*?" Hannah said. "And just how does one get a feeling like that?"

So it was on this day, after Tom let her read the letters, that Hannah had resolved to find a gift with as much shimmering complexity as Sydney's words. The clock was ticking, and she could think of nothing.

She spent all Saturday morning brainstorming. There were only two days to go. She had succeeded in creating expectations of such superhuman heights that by the time Tom left to play basketball with some friends at 12:30, she felt quite unable to leave the house. It was all she could do to slap together some Christmas-cookie dough and stick it in the oven. Lying on her bed, staring at the ceiling, she decided to play an exercise DVD to get her heart beating again.

Halfway through, the doorbell buzzed. Although she wasn't expecting anyone, she was grateful for an interruption just as the routine was reaching its absurd zenith. Maybe a neighbor needed to borrow a measuring cup. She opened the door, jogging in place, only to discover a beautiful woman standing in the hallway with a package in her hands. A disturbingly beautiful woman.

"Hello," the woman said. "Are you Hannah?"

"I am," said Hannah, still jogging.

"I'm Sydney. I'm . . . friends with Tom." Luckily, Hannah was cardiovascularly prepared for fight-or-flight. Sydney took a breath. "I hate to bother you like this, but I was back in town for the holidays, and I knew Tom's birthday was Monday, and I . . . well, to be honest, I didn't make it to the post office in time. I keep forgetting that in Boston, things actually *close*."

Hannah stopped jogging. So this fresh-faced, long-legged thing was Sydney.

"I'm really sorry to bother you," Sydney said. "I just wanted to drop this off."

The package was wrapped in brown paper marked with a hurried address—in red ink, of course. Hannah put it on the counter and wiped her hands on the front of her yoga pants. She would greet her reckoning with as much dignity as she could muster, wearing spandex.

"Come on in," she said.

She offered Sydney a chair, but before she herself sat down, she ran to silence the DVD player, where a bald man was shouting something about inner thighs much too loudly for an occasion like this. When she returned, she found Sydney glancing about the apartment.

"Tom's out for the afternoon," she said, deciding at the last minute to leave off the "I'm afraid" part.

"Yeah, no, I—"

"What'd you get him?" she asked, jerking her head toward the package. She couldn't hold out any longer.

"Oh, it's an Angry Salad CD. They're this band." Sydney's face opened up. "Actually, they're amazing. Completely new. With really thoughtful lyrics. They have that edge-of-the-planet kind of feel."

*Edge of the planet?* Hannah wondered if Columbus had for some reason fallen out of fashion among the fresh young writing pack.

"You might like them," Sydney said.

Hannah found this highly unlikely, especially since she was considering throwing *them* into the trash as soon as Sydney's pretty little ponytail was out the door.

Sydney leaned in closer. "I take it back. You'll love them," she said. She touched Hannah's forearm. "I give you my word."

Hannah smelled fire. The cookies! She ran to the stove and pulled on a zebra-striped oven mitt.

"This is embarrassing," she said. She was going to have things to talk about in therapy for the next year and a half. The sugary green trees were seconds shy of ruination. "Care for a cookie?"

"Sure," Sydney said. She selected one of the least charred. "Thanks."

Hannah watched Sydney's mouth as she chewed. She had full lips and almost imperceptible dimples.

"I usually need a little something to cancel out the exercise," Hannah said.

Sydney laughed and pressed her fingertips into some crumbs that had fallen on the table. "You make a mean cookie," she said, and for the next half hour, the two women talked with what could only be described as surprising ease, considering they were both in love with the same man.

"I should probably get going," Sydney said, brushing off the tops of her jeans and standing up. "Thanks for everything."

"My pleasure," said Hannah. Then, when she went to put the milk away, Sydney shocked her while her back was turned.

"I could tell from the things Tom said about you," Sydney said, while Hannah stared at orange juice and casserole and pickles. "I just knew you'd be lovely."

When Tom came home, at 4:15, Hannah was in the shower. He opened the bathroom door and steam spilled into the hallway.

"Hey there, Lulu," he said. "Mind if I join?"

"Feel free," Hannah said. He pulled off his T-shirt and stepped out of his shorts.

"A package came for you this afternoon," she said.

"Oh yeah?" he said, peeling off his socks.

"Yeah," Hannah said. And his underwear. "A birthday present."

He slid the shower curtain aside and admired a bouquet of foam sliding down her back. She stepped out from under the stream of water and kissed him on the cheek.

"It was dropped off in person," she said. "From Sydney," she added, and handed him the bar of soap.

Underneath it all, Hannah was a firm believer in letting people do what they want. Many of her friends, who had previously seemed perfectly sane, had in the past couple of years started talking an awful lot about bait-cutting and cow-buying. But to Hannah, it seemed that forcing things only led to the most Pyrrhic of victories: the captive sparrow, twitching in your hand, limp with defeat; or the pacing tiger, remaining out of dry duty, parched and angered by his own obligation. Ultimately she was only out for her own best interest: She wanted the pleasure of being with someone she knew freely, in his deepest heart, wanted to be with her. If Tom chose to run off with his little correspondent, so be it. Hannah just wanted to be sure that before he left, he knew her for the generous and clever creature she truly was.

That night, a thick, soft snow fell, muffling the rooftops of the city with cashmere quiet. Hannah had a dream. It was summer; she was flying over the house she grew up in, in Maine. There was no roof; she could see into her childhood bedroom. Tom and Sydney were in it, dancing.

Sydney was kissing him, touching him. She kept pausing and looking up at Hannah.

*This? Like this? Is this okay?*

Hannah kept trying to communicate down to her: *Yes—yes. Just like that.*

Sydney put her lips against Tom's neck. He closed his eyes. She slid her hand under his waistband. He was falling. Wait—stop. Where was Hannah? He couldn't breathe; he was going to suffocate. "Hannah!" he cried.

*It's all right,* Hannah said, concentrating. *I see you. I love you.*

Sydney was with Tom, and Hannah was in tune with Sydney. When she finally took hold of him, in a swift, firm grip, his head fell back as a wave of pleasure passed through his body. And up in the sky, Hannah felt the pleasure, too.

The next morning, while Tom was in the shower, she went to the phone book and called Sydney.

"I have an idea," she said.

"Let me see if I have this straight." Nihan was highly amused. "It doesn't count as cheating if you're in the same room, naked." Hannah hoped she knew what she was doing. "And what exactly is your role in this bacchanalian jamboree going to be?"

"I don't know," Hannah said. "We didn't write a script. I just told her to bring a couple of bottles of wine."

"And the young Thomas doesn't know this is going to happen?"

"No."

"You'd better make that three bottles."

Hannah felt a jab of doubt. She was still uneasy about scheduling dates for Tom's penis without consulting him first. "Do you think he'll mind?"

"Honey," Nihan said, draping an arm across her friend's shoulders, "this has been every man's fantasy since he learned to count to three. No. I don't think he'll mind."

Hannah and Sydney had found planning the logistics to be somewhat difficult. They discussed hiding Sydney in the closet with a glass of wine and the door cracked open so she'd get enough air. They joked around about using such lines as: "Okay, Tom, now you let us take care of everything," or "Just let us know if the blindfold is too tight." Hannah figured it wouldn't be funny if she lost her nerve right when they all took off their clothes and said something like: "Just kidding!" There really was no getting out of it now. Well, maybe the joke would be on them: Tom would take the opportunity to announce he was gay, and she wouldn't have to go through with it.

Monday, December 22, 2008. The day Thomas Groff turned twenty-six. The day he would remember on his deathbed.

Sydney was hiding in the bedroom, with the cake. She and Hannah had decided to surprise Tom by emerging together, with the lights down and the birthday candles lit. The bedroom was right off of the kitchen, so Hannah could slip in for "the cake" whenever. Depending on how much wine they'd had, the two of them might or might not quickly strip down to their underwear. They were waiting to decide that on the spur of the moment, feeling much too sober at present to make such an important decision. Besides, Tom was expected any minute. Before he arrived, they opened a spare bottle of Champagne so they could make a toast together.

"To surprises," Hannah said.

When Tom walked through the door she went to hug him, but his arms were behind his back. When she stepped away, he produced roses. Three. She thought, for one terrifying instant, that he'd divined her plan, but of course he hadn't. He'd just gotten lucky.

"You've got it backwards, darling," she said, beaming. "Your birthday is when *I* give *you* the gifts, remember?"

"I know," he said, passing the flowers from one hand to the other as he pulled out of his winter coat. "But the genius on the corner knows a sucker when he sees one."

She helped with the coat and was about to go looking for a vase for the flowers when he took everything out of her hands and put it all on the counter.

"Come here," he said, arms wide. He pulled her to his chest and held her. "You're so good to me, baby," he said. "You're the reason I'm glad I was born."

Hannah was grateful he couldn't see her face. She was so giddy with excitement, so close to bursting with secret anticipation, that she was sure her expression would have given her surprise away.

Sydney had been observing this scene from the bedroom, where she was crouched in the dark—like a burglar, out in the night, peering in someone else's warmly lit windows, waiting in the bushes for the chance to sneak in. To rob them. She may have felt afraid, touched by what she'd just witnessed and knowing that everything could change after something like this. She might have felt guilty, recognizing that it was she who had everything to gain and Hannah who had everything to lose. For whatever reason, she stood up and hurried for the door.

"I'm sorry," she said, rushing past them and out of the apartment. "Bye."

Hannah couldn't believe her eyes. Neither could Tom.

"I'll be right back," Hannah said, pressing her palm to his chest.

"Sydney, wait!" she said. But Sydney didn't stop. She

was already halfway down the hall and within reach of the exit. "What's wrong? Hold on for a second, wait!"

When Sydney stopped walking, Hannah realized how desperately she wanted her to come back. And this was how she knew she had succeeded in finding the perfect gift. She had stepped into the kind of gesture that, like all inspired unselfish acts, had left her feeling more like she was receiving something than like she was giving something away.

Sydney stopped walking and turned around. Her eyes reflected the sad yellow light of the hallway.

"What's the matter?" Hannah said. She tilted her head. "C'mon. Come here."

"I don't know," Sydney said. She opened her mouth, then closed it. Hannah was walking toward her. She tried again. "It's just—he really loves you, you know?"

Before she could get to the rest, Hannah had taken her hand and was leading her back to the apartment. "March!" she said, stomping her feet. Tipsy and determined, she pulled Sydney—reluctant still, but willing to be led.

When they reached the doorway, Hannah stopped abruptly and Sydney bumped up against her back. With Sydney right behind her, she put her key in the lock, but before she opened it, she turned. She turned around, and she kissed Sydney, kissed her soft, warm lips.

It was a delicate, grateful, exciting kiss, and when she pulled away, Sydney's eyes were still closed.

"I knew you'd be lovely," Hannah said, and opened the door.

# PROOF OF LOVE

Kelly loved Jesus, and she also loved Nash. Well, she didn't love Nash exactly, but she found him to be very intriguing. She felt she *could* love him. Nash worked at Whole Foods and had blue eyes that were so pale and bright they almost looked fake. She'd spotted him there five months ago, and they chatted while she was helping him bag the food. He held up her salsa.

"Watch yourself, this one's industrial strength."

"I keep cayenne pepper in my glove compartment," she said. "You can't get too spicy for me."

"In your glove compartment."

"For spice emergencies," she said.

The following week she caught herself reapplying her lipstick before she went in and waiting until his line was open to approach the cash registers.

"These look good," he said, scanning a box of coconut ice creams frozen in the half shell.

"They're from France," Kelly said. "They do things like that in France."

He smiled. "Indeed they do."

"I don't even like ice cream," she said. "I just liked the looks of them."

"You don't like ice cream? What is that, some kind of birth defect or something?"

"We've all got our flaws," she said.

A week and a half later she bought two bottles of wine. In line, she admitted that the salesmen at her local wineshop intimidated her. "It's not just the jargon; it's the way they seem so enlightened or something. Like they've shed all attachment to material things."

"All except the grape," he said.

"Well, if you're going to grant exceptions, the grape is a great place to start." She pretended to read his name off his shirt, but really she'd noted it weeks ago. "And you, Nash? Have you given up all earthly attachments?"

"Uh, my answer to that would have to be an unqualified no."

"Care to help me out with one of these?"


They got drunk on her back porch. It was the last balmy night of summer. Her dog loved him, sat in his lap, wouldn't leave him alone. She was a graphic artist for a magazine, and her dog's name was Pixel. She told him both these things, which were true. She also told him that she didn't like her job very much, which wasn't true.

"If I ever get fired, I'm coming to work at Whole Foods. If you people will have me, that is."

"I don't know—they're very selective. They can tell if you're only in it for the discount."

"Well, I wouldn't *turn down* the discount," she said. She took a sip of her wine. "You know, in Atlanta, they call Whole Foods 'Whole Paycheck.'" The previous weekend she'd left Chicago for Atlanta to visit her sister. Kelly was older than Michelle, but because Michelle had married and was procreating close to their parents' home in Buckhead, where they'd grown up, she was openly favored. Kelly was the only one in her family of science types who practiced the faith, a faith she'd learned on the sly from her Catholic grandmother, and for this and other reasons she was considered the odd duck in the family. The black sheep. The wet chicken.

She noticed their glasses were empty and went to fetch another bottle. "How'd you end up working there?" she said.

"Lack of ambition," Nash said flatly. "The usual things don't inspire me."

"And which things might those be?"

"You know—money. Fame. Power." There was no hint of reprimand in his voice even though the answer now seemed obvious.

Kelly refilled their glasses, giving the bottle a little half-twist at the end. "So what *does* inspire you?" she said. She knew what she wanted him to say: Love. Truth. Beauty. But Nash didn't answer. "You don't fool me," she said, sitting back down. "I bet you secretly want to rule the world. I'm sure you have your plans." But Nash just looked at her with his sea blue eyes and said nothing.

"What's with all the God stuff?" he asked, indicating

her wall with a lift of his chin. There was a profile of Jesus to the left of her fireplace, and next to the window hung some giant ivory rosary beads she'd picked up in Mexico. On various shelves and tables there were figurines, prayer cards, scapulars. She hadn't intended her decor to have a religious theme; it had just ended up that way.

"What can I say? I love the guy."

"What guy?"

"Jesus."

"Rrright," said Nash. "Jesus."

"I'm very religious," Kelly said. "But not in the usual way." It was true. Kelly was not formal with God. "Baby," she called him, as in, "Jesus, baby, you're the one for me." She deeply suspected God was a lot funnier and more hip than people gave him credit for. Everyone was always so lugubrious: the capital letters, the hair shirts. She tried to put herself in God's shoes. What would she want? Tenderness, intimacy. An unparalleled love. Someone whose loyalty was independent of circumstance. Someone who tried to be original, in addition to reciting prayers. So that's what she tried to give. Doing the dishes, ambling through the supermarket, she tossed little nuggets his way: "I love you, G. What's not to love?" She tried to keep it fresh and simple.

Her friend Gwen told her she was insane. Kelly thought this was harsh. "You could say *eccentric* and get your point across. You could say *intense*." But to be honest, she'd learned not to expect others to understand. At times, people in the pew beside her would begin to nod when the priest said something counterintuitive, such as that gays had no place in the kingdom of heaven, or that birth control was a sin. She heard what the priest was saying, but something inside her didn't believe it. She couldn't imagine those words on Jesus' lips. "I'm sorry," she would whisper. "We don't really know what we're doing here—we need help. We need you." She stole jokes from movies like *Jerry Maguire*. "Help us to help you. Help us to help you help us."

The air was thick with silence; Nash was waiting for her to speak. "I think the church gets a lot of things wrong," she said. "It's man who makes a fuss over what people do with their genitals. God cares more what people do with their hearts."

"The church gets more wrong than it gets right, if you ask me," Nash said. "The Crusades. The Spanish Inquisition."

"Yeah, well, Jesus is wildly misunderstood and always has been. What can I say?" She paused. "You should give him a chance."

Nash laughed. "First of all, you don't know what I have or haven't given him. Maybe I have given him a chance."

"You should give him a second chance."

Nash took a long drink of his wine. "I didn't know you were a Jesus freak," he said. "You don't seem all that conservative."

"I thought it was hilarious when the church said it was choosing a conservative pope, to remain true to its roots. Jesus was a radical."

"You are right about that, I suppose."

She felt encouraged by this concession, minor though it was. "C'mon," she said. "Give the guy another chance."

"You think you have it all figured out, don't you?" he said.

"No," Kelly said. She could feel the wine's heat in her cheeks. "Not really." She set down her glass and leaned closer to him. "But I secretly want to save the world," she said.

He slipped a loose strand of hair behind her ear. "It's not so secret," he said.

At the end of the night, he didn't kiss her—not even on the cheek. Nor did he kiss her when he rode his bike over two weeks later, although he did bring a jar of blackberry preserves, and tell her stories about how he'd been a philosophy major at Northwestern but had spent most of his time doing laps in the pool. He said it helped unclog his head. "The problem with philosophers is that most of them can't write clearly," he said. "I'd get to the end of a sentence that went on for a paragraph and realize I didn't know what the verb was."

"I know what you mean," Kelly said. She toasted sesame-seed bagels for the jam and asked him to pick out some music. It was late afternoon, but ample sunlight still slanted through the windows of her kitchen. She could hear the neighborhood kids playing in the street. On weekdays, Chicago felt like a city, but on Sundays, it always felt like a small town.

"Don't you have any jazz?" he asked, thumbing through her CDs.

"I wish I liked jazz, because I think it's sort of cool to like, but actually I hate it. All that meandering around . . . It's depressing."

Nash was shaking his head. "There's no real hope for you. You know that, right?"

"I know," she said, spreading jam on a bagel. "I'm a misfit. I also hate zoos and baths. And pesto."

"That's a lot of hate for one so young," he said, which she took as a compliment. She was thirty-six, and figured Nash to be at least a couple of years her junior. He selected an Ellis Paul CD. "What have you got against baths, anyway?"

"They're so *boring*. It's just being stationary and wet. You try to read, but the book gets all soggy. And the water gets cold. Then you get this crick in your neck, and you can never quite get comfortable—"

"At least now I know what to do if we ever need to torture you—forced bath time," he said. She loved his face; there was always a measure of sadness in it, even when he was smiling.

"How's Baby been treating you?" he said. Baby had become their code word for Jesus.

"Baby always treats me right," she said. "Next Monday is Yom Kippur, so I'll be fasting, like he would have done." Kelly had such respect for Judaism and so liked to remind people of Jesus' Jewishness that her boss had taken to calling her "Jesus for Jews over here." She set the plate in front of Nash. "On an entirely unrelated note, could I interest you in a mimosa?"

He looked pleased. "Twist my arm," he said.

She dug a bottle out from the back of the fridge. "I have this Champagne a friend brought me from a wedding she went to. I guess she felt bad because she'd called me at four in the morning to ask what brevity was the soul of. She was working on her toast, and just drew a blank." She could feel Nash's eyes on the back of her neck.

"If brevity's the soul of wit, what's verbosity the soul of?" he said.

She shrugged.

"Tenure," he said.

"That's a good one."

"My mom's a professor," he said. "She hates the bullshit."

She handed him a mimosa and held up her glass. "To a world with less bullshit," she said, to which he quickly added, "and other things that will never happen."

"We need a revolution," she said. "A less-bullshit revolution."

Nash swallowed the sweet concoction and fake winced, as if he'd taken a hit of grappa. "'All revolutions evaporate, leaving only the slime of bureaucracy,'" he said.

"Ain't it the truth."

"That's Kafka, of course. Not me."

"Gotta love Kafka," Kelly said. "We could use a few more Kafkas around here." She set her glass on the table and they both sat down. "What does your mom teach?"

"Psychiatry. She's at the med school."

"Oh," Kelly said. "Free therapy." Nash raised an eyebrow as if to say that free therapy from your mother is not something you want.

"How about your dad?" she said. Her own father was a molecular engineer, and was as honest and gentle as they came. He fell into a category of large-hearted nonbelievers whom she privately referred to as the Christlike non-Christians.

"My father killed himself when I was eleven," Nash said.

"I'm so sorry," she said softly. She had the impulse to touch him, but her arms felt as if they belonged to someone else. "What was he like?"

"I consider him to have been a professional sloganeer. He always had these sayings, like: *Do today's work today* and *Neither hurry nor wait.* Or my mom's favorite: *Keep your words soft and tender, for tomorrow you might have to eat them.* I don't remember that much about him, to be honest. He used to read me Shakespeare's plays as bedtime stories. Then he would stub his toe and say: 'Fie on't!' and I would laugh."

"He sounds wonderful."

Nash drained his glass. "Sometimes life just doesn't make sense, I guess."

"But we only see partially," Kelly said. "We don't see how it all plays out."

"No, I can tell you how it played out: He's dead."

"Right, but—"

He stood up and placed his hand on top of her head. "Sorry, kiddo, but I should hit the road," he said, and before she knew it, he'd pushed open the door, swung a leg over his bike, and was pedaling away.

"I love him," Kelly said. She and Gwen were having mochaccinos at an outdoor café and watching people pass by on their way to the independent movie theater or the

Armenian restaurant. "I want to take his clothes off with my teeth."

"He still hasn't kissed you? Nothing?"

"Nada. It's like he's never heard of kissing. And I'm afraid to touch him. I can't tell if it would be welcome."

"How often does he come over?"

"Once a week. For the past two months."

"And he calls you every other day?"

"Yup."

"And he's not gay?"

"Nope."

Gwen stirred her whipped cream dispiritedly with a flat wooden stick. She seemed to be wearying of the Nash subject. "What do you even like about this guy?"

Kelly looked down at her coffee. "He has interesting observations. He doesn't care about unimportant things."

"Like showering and shaving?"

She lifted her chin. "He stands a little apart from the world. I like that."

"He seems a little broken, in my opinion."

"We're all a little broken."

Gwen rolled her eyes. "Lucky for him you're drawn to the hopeless ones. You and your bleeding heart."

Kelly knew she had some radical ideas concerning heaven. "I've heard that in heaven, my joy will be complete. And my joy will be incomplete unless everyone comes with me," she told her priest. This was during confession, when she was supposed to be focusing on her own sins. She half-expected the priest to say: "Well, now that you mention it, little lady, you do have a point there." He didn't. But neither did he protest.

It was Gwen who protested. "Even the bad guys get to go—the killers and the rapists?"

Kelly stood her ground.

"Even the people who don't, you know, believe in Jesus?" Gwen was not particularly religious, and her mouth always got a bit gummy when saying the word *Jesus* out loud.

"If faith is a gift, how can you punish those who don't have it?"

Gwen paused. "What good is heaven if everyone gets to go? What justice is there in that?"

"Mercy is greater than justice," Kelly said. She believed it with all her heart.

On Sunday morning she went to church. She'd just learned the Spanish word for *mercy* and thought it was beautiful, found herself repeating it under her breath as she drove. *Misericordia, misericordia.* During the Gospel reading, the priest said, "May all who have ears hear," to which Kelly quickly prayed, "Give everybody ears." At the end of Mass it was announced that there would be a prayer vigil at five o'clock to end abortion. Kelly always wondered why they didn't have prayer vigils to end unwanted pregnancy, and had once put this idea in what she thought was a suggestion box but turned out to be a donation box for the world's poor. She stayed late, alone in the empty pews, and prayed. She felt Jesus close, as she often did—invisible but close. This was her life: always sensing him and missing him at the same time.

She wanted to pray about Nash, who indeed seemed

to keep separate from the world, and she was beginning to fear that she was part of the world he kept separate from. But she tried to be careful never to tell God what to do. Instead of praying for a Cubs victory, for instance, she simply said: "May your holy will be done." Then later, she chastised herself: *Well, maybe you should have been a little more* specific.

"Make my heart your heaven," she said. She lowered her head. "I give you my life." She wished she had something better to give; she knew she was no model of blind obedience. "I offer you the lives of all the saints," she said. She liked the way the communion of saints allowed you to share in the good works of others. "I offer you all the love of all time. Give me everything you want me to have, even if there's suffering involved."

She had to admit, she had not yet learned the art of loving suffering. She realized she should; she knew suffering was proof of love. "Do you know that the saints in heaven would envy you?" she'd once read in a mystic's diary she found in her grandmother's closet. "Their time of sacrifice is over." She thought she understood what this meant. Now, while she had free will, was her chance to show God she loved him more than earthly things. Nevertheless, she found herself avoiding sacrifice and seeking her own pleasure. She tried to override this tendency—the tendency toward self-satisfaction, when she could be trying to charm God—but it was difficult. Still, she knew God understood this difficulty. God understood everything.

. . .

"Hey, you," Nash said, tapping her screen. It was Saturday night, and the setting sun had turned the sky into a Cheryl Wheeler lyric: *drop jaw red, Maxfield Parrish blue.* Three weeks had gone by since she'd last seen him.

"Hi," she said brightly. "Where've you been?"

"No questions," he said. "I want to take you somewhere. Come with me."

Whole Foods was locked up for the night, but he had a key. While Nash led, she followed behind with her hands on his shoulders. Even in the dark, she knew what they were passing: Straight ahead was the table with gingerbread loaves and tangerine cookies; to the left were the shelves with sun-dried tomato pesto and imported cornichons; to the right were the goat cheese and salad greens.

When they reached the back of the store, he sat down on the mottled linoleum. "There's something I've wanted to tell you," he said. His hands moved restlessly in his lap. As soon as she sat down beside him, he stood up. "It's hard to explain," he said. In the light from the rows of refrigerated milk, his face looked almost pellucid.

"I went to my father's grave. I hadn't been there for a long time," he said. "I was lying on the ground, right above where he's buried, when I noticed this stone angel on top of a monument, way up high. She was holding a horn in one hand, and her other hand was open at her side. And she's staring at the sky, like she's listening for something, or waiting for something." He'd been pacing, but now he stopped. "Do you know what I mean? Like she's listening for a music she has yet to hear."

"Maybe God—"

"No!" he said. "This has nothing to do with God. What I'm trying to say here doesn't have anything to do with God!"

She didn't know what to say. He'd never raised his voice to her before.

"It has to do with me," he said.

Her eyes were fixed on the rows of milk. "I just thought—"

"Forget it," he said. "Forget I ever said anything." In his face she saw a hint of something else, and she wondered what it was she was supposed to forget. He turned and headed for the exit. "Let's get out of here."

Kelly's disappointment emboldened her. "You always come close and then run away," she said to his back, still sitting Indian-style on the floor. "Why is that?" Nash kept walking. "Why'd you even bring me here?" He was out of sight now, but she could hear the sound of metal on metal, and for a second it crossed her mind that he could lock her in for the night. But he wouldn't do that. Would he?

"Nash!" she said, addressing the idea of Nash, his wraith. "What is it you want from me?"

When she got up, she would discover that the door was unlocked, but Nash was long gone. She figured she had her answer.


So it was over. It was over before it began, which made it even harder to take. Kelly was surprised by how much it affected her. She couldn't concentrate at work; she avoided Gwen; she kept checking her messages for the apology that never came. She didn't like to second-guess God, but considering how things had turned out, she couldn't help wondering what the point had been of meeting Nash in the first place.

It had been raining for days. Pouring. Fortunately, Kelly had recently had the roof reshingled, or there would have been a swamp in her living room. She brewed a pot of chamomile tea and pretended to ignore the banging sound of the loose drainpipe. Until she couldn't pretend any longer. She grabbed her coat and switched on the outside lights, not sure what her plan was but figuring she ought to do something. As soon as she stepped outside, she saw him. He was standing in the middle of her front lawn, in the rain.

"Nash," she said. She was quiet inside, almost frightened. "What are you doing?"

"I'm thinking," he said. "I guess you might call it praying." His voice sounded different, and she noticed he wasn't wearing any shoes.

"Why don't you come inside?" she said. "You can pray in here."

His eyes tightened. "I was just wondering—*praying*," he said again, but he'd given the word a certain meanness, "how a benevolent God can allow so much *suffering*." He made a sweeping gesture on the word *suffering*, and she wondered if he was maybe drunk. "It's a simple question, don't you think? And I'm going to stand right here till I get an answer."

Pixel whimpered at her feet, wanting to run to him.

"We don't always get answers our way, in our time," she said. "It doesn't work like that."

"It does tonight." He gave her a look that suggested he was ready to stand on her lawn for the rest of his life, and for a moment she imagined him there, patches of snow resting on his shoulders like a statue's, dandelions sprouting through his toes in the spring.

"God suffers the most," she said. "He only keeps himself hidden out of respect for our free will."

"Bull-*shit!*" Nash said, rainwater spraying from his lips. "You want a less-bullshit revolution? That's ironic. You are the queen of bullshit. And you know what else? Not only is it bullshit, it's the most milquetoasty, goody-goody, meaningless bullshit I've ever heard. Sometimes I'm amazed that you can say the things you do with a straight face."

Kelly was stunned. To her, they'd always felt like a team, even when they disagreed, like those celebrity couples who argue politics on TV. It had never occurred to her that he was secretly repulsed. A flurry of comebacks flashed through her mind: *Why don't you stay home then? Why keep coming here if I'm so disgusting?* But the sting of his words left her speechless. She went back inside, slamming the door behind her as hard as she could. In her bedroom, she stood to one side of the window so he couldn't see her watching him. She knew she wanted him to come in after her. She also knew he never would.

By the time she went back outside, he was kneeling in the mud. He didn't look up when she said his name, didn't acknowledge her at all. She got down beside him.

"Nash," she said.

When he lifted his face, it was laced with sorrow. "Why?" he said. His hands were fists in the grass. "Why why why why why why?"

"I don't know," she said. "I don't have all the answers. Sometimes I just like to act as if I do."

He pulled an amber-colored bottle from his pocket. "Know what these are?" he said, rattling it. "These are the antidepressants I've been taking for the last, oh, ten years. They're supposed to dampen my desire to kill myself. And guess what? They also dampen everything else, if you know what I mean. Make it pretty much impossible." He met her eyes. "Still feel like hanging around?" He stuck the bottle back in his pocket. "Allow me to answer for you."

"Come on, let's go inside."

"No," he said. "Your God has some explaining to do. I've waited long enough. I'm tired of waiting."

She didn't want to argue with him. She felt rather tired herself. Tired of the waiting, and the misunderstanding; tired for what's lost, and what's never held in the first place. Tired for all the music that slips by unheard. She put her fingers beneath his chin.

Across the street, the neighbors turned out their light, and a garage door slowly hummed to a close. In the end, there was no answer. There was no thunder, there was no lightning from the sky. There was just a woman, kneeling in her yard in the rain, and a man, lifting his face, waiting to be kissed.

# WE'VE GOT A GREAT

# FUTURE BEHIND US

"Allow me to declare this a disaster in advance." Zeb is standing in the entrance to the Oak Bar at the Hermitage Hotel, holding a guitar case and a carry-on. I rise from my chair, abandoning a laptop, a highball, and the plans I've been making to cover the following contingencies: Zeb misses his flight, Zeb shows up with a showgirl, Zeb shows up drunk, Zeb shows up with a drunk showgirl, Zeb sends a man dressed as a singing gorilla to take his place. His glance has a sideways cast, and I know he's looking for Debra-Lynn.

"She's already up in the room," I say. "I thought it might be best if you and I had ourselves a cocktail first."

"I'm telling you, Walt, this whole idea is a mistake," he says. "She will sabotage any project she's associated with. Her only joy is the misery of others. The woman has a tabloid heart."

I pull out a chair, and he sits. "That attitude isn't going to make things any easier," I say.

"Easier? Nothing in heaven, hell, or anywhere in between is going to make this any easier," he says, picking up the cocktail menu. He takes out his glasses, and I can't help but wonder how much of my predicament shows on my face. I haven't had a hit song since 1998, and I'm on the most-wanted list of seven different collection agents, not to mention my possibly mob-affiliated landlord. But that's not the best part, the new part.

"I wasn't going to tell you this," I say.

"You always say that whenever you're about to tell me something anyway."

"Catherine's pregnant."

Zeb whumps the table. "Well, what do you know. How did that happen?"

"So her tapped-out credit cards and my puny honorariums aren't going to cut it anymore."

"Honorariums?" he says. "You get those?" While I'm trying to get him to pay attention, his only concern is flagging down the waitress. Before he and Deb got hitched, whenever we finished a set, his first words were always the same: "Where is the booze and where are the women?"

I take his hand and look him in the eye. "We're on a mission here," I say. "A very important mission."

Back when I used to do the festival circuit with Zeb and Deb, as their opening act—back when everything they touched turned platinum—they promised they'd collaborate with me on a song. So now, even though they haven't spoken to each other in over two years, even though it's practically a violation of a restraining order for them to be in the same state, I'm calling in my chits, asking for the favor. Maybe it's insanity, but maybe it's my only hope.

Zeb gives up on the waitress and finishes my highball for me. "Did I ever tell you about the time she convinced herself I was cheating on her, and cut the crotch out of every pair of pants I owned?"

"Let's try to stay focused," I say. "We don't have time to wallow in the past."

"I have more fun there," he says. He slaps a pack of cigarettes on the table so they'll be ready when he needs them. "Perhaps we should discuss my fee," he says. We hadn't discussed his fee because I hadn't considered paying him a fee. Springing for a weekend at the toniest hotel in Nashville seemed fee enough.

"I'll be paying you in gin and tonics," I say, and finally catch the eye of Sally, a bare-armed brunette with a honeysuckle voice.

"Not even an honorarium?" he says. A slow smile spreads across his face. "My fee is that you name the kid after me."

I have no idea if he's serious. Zebulon got his name not from the Bible, nor from Zebulon Pike—who never actually reached the summit of Pikes Peak—but from a poker game. His mother, eight months pregnant, was standing at his father's elbow when his father lost a final hand to a pair of nines, held by a man named Zebulon Smith. This was the nadir of a long losing streak, during which the young couple had mortgaged nearly everything they owned. The victor, perhaps in a moment of pity, had agreed to let them off the hook on one condition: The unborn child would bear his name.

"You're joking," I say.

"I am serious as whiskers on a shark."

"Zeb, remember, the pregnancy's a secret," I say. "No one's supposed to know. And I'm having a lot of trouble with the whole marriage idea." When I first told Catherine I saw conventional life, the standard white-picket-fence thing—marriage—as a bit of a trap, she said: "Have you ever considered that the unmarried, unconventional life is *also* a trap?"

"Just name the kid after me, and I'll give this my best shot," Zeb says. "No—I will *deliver.*"

In the old days, back when they were the barn-burning, show-stopping success story of the lower forty-eight, the mighty duo could whip off an award-winning song in their sleep. Zebulon and Debra-Lynn were the top of the heap. They'd played everywhere, from the Louisiana Hayride to the Grand Ole Opry herself. Their love songs, and their love story, were legendary; there wasn't a waitress in all of Nashville who hadn't heard of Zeb & Deb. High school sweethearts, separated by fate, reunited in a guitar shop on Nashville's Lower Broadway. For a while everything seemed perfect, like the sappy ending to a country love song. Marital bliss, material success, fame from bridge to bridge. Then came the kind of divorce you read about in gossip magazines, with a mean-spiritedness as outlandish as the love it had replaced. Recording-studio vendettas, pet custody battles, even an alleged poisoning attempt. It was payback for every corny love song they'd ever written. No: It was

as if they were atoning for every hack lyricist since someone first rhymed *moon* and *June*. After breaking up their
act, neither one had succeeded in bottling the lightning
solo. Gradually they retreated from the public eye, and
appeared to have quit writing altogether. Until now. I
hoped.

In the elevator, Zeb stares at his boots.

"I realize you haven't seen each other in a while," I say.

"Buddy, I'm way ahead of you. I brought my airsick
bag from the plane." He pulls a neat, square bag out of
his back pocket, and I feel a bizarre surge of nausea.

"I'm telling you," he says. "If she pulls any of her
funny business, I can't be held—"

"She won't. She won't, I promise. In fact, she told me
she's sorry—for everything that happened. At the end."

"You're lying."

"Okay, I'm lying," I say. "But please—*please*. Let's
just try to get through the next forty-eight hours as pain-
lessly as we can."

"I don't think that's possible," he says. "I don't mind
telling you, I think the entire cosmos is against us here."

When we get to the door to the room, we both just
stand there. It took a titanic amount of wheedling to
make this reunion happen, but now that the hour has arrived, I want to run. I force myself to give a single rap
with my middle knuckle.

"Deb?" No answer. Zeb eyeballs the room-service
tray she's left on the floor, where there's a linen napkin
with a triangle of steak peeking out.

"See? Carnivore," he whispers, just as Deb opens the door. She's wearing a silky green dress, and her lips have that magazine-ad sheen. Deb's pushing fifty but could pass for thirty-five. Zeb's pushing fifty but could pass for sixty.

"Well, hello," she says to me. She doesn't look at Zeb.

"Hello, beauty," I say. We kiss each other on the cheek as I enter, and the door shuts behind us, leaving Zeb out in the hallway. I squeeze Deb's hands. "Hold that thought," I say.

Zeb is frozen where I left him. "I can't do it," he says. "She's too toxic. I don't think I can be in the same room with her."

I am a grown man, thirty-nine years old, from a seventh-generation Southern family. But I am not proud. I drop to my knees and gaze up at him.

"You promised me you would deliver," I say.

Zeb reaches into his coat pocket, pulls out one of those miniature booze bottles they give you on airplanes, and tilts it back. Then he lifts me by my armpits, and we go in.

The three of us settle around a coffee table where Deb has set out a ceramic pot and two teacups. No one says anything; Zeb and Deb have yet to make eye contact. From my backpack I pull out some sheets of paper and hand each of them a pencil.

"So," I say. I hold my pencil purposefully, as if to set an example. I've never been much of a leader—"Born Follower" was my hit song from 1998—but I know I'm the captain of this doomed misadventure. Captain McGlue.

"I thought we'd try to write something hysterically

funny, but also heartbreaking, with some unexpected tenderness, maybe toward the end. But not at all maudlin. That rhymes."

"Jumping Jesus!" says Zeb. His face has an expression of such profound disappointment that for a second, he reminds me of my father. I flip over the page on which I've written: *Exact nature of hilarity yet to be determined.*

"What you need to do at the outset is try to write the worst horseshit you possibly can," he says.

Debra-Lynn lifts her bone white teacup and takes a sip. "And you just might succeed," she says. Her lips form a perfect polite-society smile.

Zeb glares at me. His face says mutiny. My face says mercy. It says: *Whatever you did for the least of these, you did for me.* It says: *All right, I'll name the kid Zebulon.*

"Some people build entire careers," Zeb says, "out of inventing new clichés. Scarce few are truly original." He's looking at me, but speaking to Deb.

Deb sets down her teacup. "Originality is just a sign of not enough information," she says. She's also looking at me. They have yet to look at each other.

"They can say what they want about me," says Zeb, "but they'll never say I pandered to the marketplace."

"Ha!" says Deb. "This from the man who wrote 'An Oddness of Ducks' and a song about a graveyard for roadkill?"

"Are you suggesting that a children's song about interesting plural nouns was pandering to the marketplace?" Now he's looking at her.

She looks at him, too. "I'm saying that in some cases,

originality is hard to come by. Not much rhymes with *flaccid*."

"As usual, my cherub, you are fantastically misinformed. *Acid, placid, Hasid*. And that's just off the top of my head—"

"Okay!" I say, slapping my thighs. "Good that we're thinking about rhymes. That's an excellent place to start." But the floodgates have been opened, and Deb cuts me off.

"Walt, do you know the moment I realized the enormity of my misjudgment in marrying Zeb? It was on our honeymoon. We were in Mexico, out to dinner at a four-star restaurant, and in between the entrée and dessert, over candlelight, the man seated to your right told me how much better the world would be if women weren't allowed to vote. You may think I'm kidding. I am not. That's the sort of thing this man—if we can even call him that—thinks is appropriate to say to his new bride. I should have up and left right then."

Zeb hops to his feet. "You always take that out of context! I was trying to make a point about rationality. Women let their emotions cloud things. That's all I was saying."

"*On our honeymoon*," Deb repeats. She's moving her hand in a flurried way that suggests she'd be holding a cigarette, if she hadn't given up smoking ten years ago.

Zeb pulls out his Pall Malls. He never gave up smoking. Deb turns to him in disgust. "You know you can't smoke those in here."

Zeb lights up, takes a drag. "Darling, if you give up

smoking, drinking, and loving, you don't actually live longer. You just feel like you do."

"Make him stop," she says to me, "or I'll leave."

"Let her go!" Zeb cries. "I wrote all the songs. She mixed the drinks. Go on, ask her. She'll tell you." He takes another Smirnoff out of his pocket—it's as if he has a clown car of them in there—and swallows its contents in one swig. Deb stares at me as he begins listing songs. "'Crazy in the Good Way'—mine. 'Gin and Tonic for the Soul'—mine. 'Lame Duck Boyfriend'—mine. 'The Big Bang of My Life.' 'Born to Be Kissed.' 'The Last Ice Cube in Hell.' 'Everything But Married.' Mine, mine, mine, mine, mine."

Deb stands up. "I'm leaving," she says. She turns to Zeb. "Way to come through for your friend."

I'm about to formulate a plea involving the souls of my dead ancestors when I have an idea. "Which one of you wrote 'Mistake'?" I say. Neither of them answers. Zeb stubs out his cigarette; Deb stands where she is. "You don't remember? Your most popular song, and you don't know which one of you wrote it?" I open Zeb's guitar case, take out his Gibson, and for lack of any better ideas, start to sing.

> *"Don't miss our fights, don't miss our yelling.*
> *Don't miss your cooking or your jokes.*
> *Don't miss the lies you were always telling,*
> *Or spending weekends with your folks.*
>
> *"But do I wish I'd never met you?*
> *Is regret what this song's made of?*

> *In spite of all the pain it gets you,*
> *It's never a mistake to love."*

I stop. "Now, can either of you stand there and honestly say you wish you'd never met?"

"Yes," they answer in unison.

Zeb squints at me incredulously. "You don't think we actually believed the crap we wrote, do you?"

Deb is standing by the door. "I did," she says. "Some of it, anyway. It wasn't all a lie for me, like it was for you."

"Oh, for God's sake, it wasn't all a lie for me! You just love to start in, don't you? You got so hysterical at the end, and I never knew where it came from."

"Well, your being a messed-up impossibly arrogant raving lunatic may have been a factor."

"Out of nowhere, you became this completely different person. Constantly insecure and suspicious."

"There's only one thing that makes a woman suspicious: a man who's fooling around."

"Do you hear the flawed logic in that statement?"

"I'm not talking about logic!"

"That's your *problem*!"

My cell phone rings. It's Catherine. "Guys, I have to take this call," I say, but they're too busy hurling insults to care. I wait until I'm out in the hall to flip open the phone.

"Have they killed each other yet?" Catherine asks.

"It's unclear whether they're going to kill each other or kill me."

"Maybe that's all they need—a common enemy."

"Well, they've got one." I pause, then figure I might as

well come out with it. "There's something I need to ask you," I say, and tell her about Zeb's baby-name idea.

"But I thought we could name him Rufus, if it's a boy," she says. "After James Agee."

"Sweetie, you don't name someone after a person's middle name."

"Why not?"

"You don't want him to start life in the middle of something, do you? He'll get there soon enough."

"Let's not talk about names till we get through the first trimester," she says. "Besides, I found a quote for you—for Zeb and Deb. It's from *The Prophet*. Hold on, here it is, I've got it: *When you are sorrowful look again in your heart, and you shall see that you are weeping for that which has been your delight.* Isn't that beautiful?"

"It is," I say. "But I just tried the country-western version a minute ago. It didn't work." On the other side of the door, I hear the sound of breaking glass. "I'll catch you later, sweets. I've got to go."


*The Prophet.* That's Catherine for you. The summer we met, we dropped acid together in a barn after crashing a party in Culpeper. She was visiting from California.

"Isn't it funny," she said, wiggling her fingers, "that we have bodies?" Indeed, it seemed hilarious. She ran her heel up my shin and told me she was editing a collection of poems titled *While We've Still Got Feet.* She was lying on her back in a white sundress, surrounded on all sides by fire-yellow straw. I remember becoming increasingly aware of an electricity all around us, as if the hay were somehow waiting to be transmuted into gold, if only I knew the right words. At the same time, I had another feeling: I wanted to crawl up Catherine's skirt. I put my head down and had a profoundly contrarian response to LSD: I fell asleep. When I woke up, she was laughing.

"Your snoring is like the sound the world will make," she said, "when it's coming to an end."

"I have allergies," I said. "And I'm surrounded by hay." But she didn't seem to care; she was having too much fun: eyes brimming with amusement, bits of golden straw flecking her dress.


When I open the door, Zeb's waving his arms as if trying to direct an emergency crash landing.

"What about the surprise party I threw for your fortieth birthday?" he says.

"Surprise," says Deb, "is inherently hostile."

He turns to me. "She threw the china at me! Everything's a cliché with her, not just her lyrics!"

"Let's ask Walt," Deb says, and immediately I think: *Let's not.* She steeples her fingers. "True or false: If Shakespeare were alive today, he'd be writing for television."

Zeb bounces on his toes. "It's so obvious! And he'd have a blog, too."

"You're such an ass," says Deb.

I don't know what to say. All I can think is: *What if Catherine and I end up like this?* Zeb and Deb loved each other once. Then they got married. Poor Catherine; I'm going to break her heart. I sit on the floor and bury my face in my hands.

"Walt, honey? Are you crying?" Deb drops to my level.

Zeb squats, too. "Everything okay there, buddy?"

"No," I mumble with my face still in my hands. "Everything is not okay. As you can see." They've stopped yelling, and for the first time all day, I have their undivided attention. I feel a twinge of conscience, but I ignore it.

"Catherine's sick," I say. "She lost the baby."

"Oh, God," Deb says softly. "Catherine's pregnant?"

"*Was* pregnant," Zeb says.

"And I lied to her," I say. "I told her I'd be on the first plane out tomorrow morning, and that she shouldn't worry, we were almost finished here anyway."

"I'm so sorry," Deb says. "Is there anything we can do?"

"As a matter of fact, there is. Do you think we could try to get one song written before they throw us out of this place? *One song?*"

We reassemble around the coffee table. I pull out my stack of paper and again pass it around. We find, to our surprise, that tragedy has united us, given us strength of purpose, the way a martyr's death galvanizes the troops. But we still don't know what to write about.

Zeb steals a glance at what Deb has scribbled and recoils in horror. "'Faded freesia'? What the hell kind of lyric is 'faded freesia'?"

"They're flowers, idiot," Deb says. "Beautiful, delicate flowers."

"No one knows what freesia looks like."

"Anyone who cares knows."

"No one cares!"

"*Freesia* sounds foreign, doesn't it, Walt? And freezing. Foreign and freezing, like Belgian endive. And what are you going to rhyme it with? With *rose,* you've got *nose, grows, throws, blows.*"

"You haven't written a line, and already your lyric is disgusting."

"Guys, can we maybe find an image that isn't a flower?" I say. "There must be one."

"The trouble with this assignment is, we lack a subject," Deb says.

Zeb takes her pencil from her and props his paper against his knee. "When in doubt, write what's right in front of you," he says. But what's right in front of us? Broken hotel china, a train-wrecked marriage, one final, desperate attempt to recapture a glory long gone. So that's what we write about. By the time we're finished, we know it's good.

"Hallelujah! Let's eat," Zeb says. But within minutes, we're arguing over where to go. It's amazing: While we're working on the song, Zeb and Deb are cordial to each other, even cooperative. But as soon as we put the pencils away, the old animosity returns. It reminds me of the famous Christmas truce of 1914, where those English and German soldiers on the Western Front sang carols together before they resumed shooting one another. And it's giving me major flashbacks to my parents' own ill-fated marriage, which they stuck out for four decades, quietly hating each other all the while.

"You two are on your own," I say. "If you were together for twenty years and can't share a table for twenty minutes, I can't help you."

I go back to my room, lock the door, and lie down on the bed with my arms and legs stretched out in every direction. We got the song written. I can't believe it. I almost feel as if I could crank out another song right here, right now, but that would require getting up, and it's much too blissful being splayed out like this. A buddy of mine back in Virginia, a splendid hipster named Marcellus, recently had me sing backup on a song he wrote called "Star Position." "When you're single, you can sleep in the star position" is the chorus. I assume he didn't write it just for me—just to taunt me, that is, because he knows how much I don't want to get married, but also how much I don't want my kid to be born illegitimate.

I just wish I didn't feel so trapped. It's not that we're not pro-choice; Catherine even volunteered at Planned Parenthood for a year before she got her first job in publishing. But when the decision was hers to make, this is what she chose. Oh, and I was the one who forgot to buy condoms that night, and also the one who wanted to have sex anyway. Although it's true: Catherine is the one aching to get married and start a family. Among her mother's last words to her were: "If you really want to meet a man and settle down, why in God's name are you living in San Francisco?"

In a way, her mother helped bring about her wish. It was because Catherine wound up spending so much time in northern Virginia, taking care of her, driving her to chemotherapy and all that, that our long-distance affair had a chance to take root. When her mother died, Catherine stayed. That was five years ago, and it didn't take us long to go through her small inheritance. Catherine doesn't make much working at a boutique publisher that acquires only about three titles a year, and I'm a good-for-nothing, washed-up, so-called singer-songwriter. Or I *was,* until this afternoon. Now not only do I have the song, but the backstory of the celebrity reunion that produced it is a publicist's fairy dust. Maybe Zeb and Deb could even be prevailed upon to get up onstage and sing it with me: "We've Got a Great Future Behind Us."

I wake a few hours later with a start, but there's nothing there. My heart's racing, and I've been sweating in my sleep. I walk over to the suitcase that's open on the luggage rack like an inhuman maw, reach into the side pocket, and pull out the box. Even the box is beautiful, black and velvety, like a night sky housing a lone star—a star so perfect, you only need one. It was Marcellus who told me about the pawnshop on Crenshaw I went to after checking in this morning. I entered with my prize possession in tow: a tenor saxophone that had been my father's and was once owned by the late, great Coleman Hawkins. I hoisted the case onto the counter and watched the owner try to hide the frisson he got when I announced what it contained.

"Well, butter my butt and call me a biscuit!" said a customer who'd overheard me speak of the sax's provenance. He was an old black man in a tweed jacket who, unlike the owner, had no reason to mute his enthusiasm. The owner was a tall man named Fred. When I asked why his shop was named Impermanence, he told me he was a Buddhist. Devout. Each time he handed me a ring and I stared at its facets, trying to see if I could envision my future among them, the old man in the tweed jacket would catch his breath. "Oh, she'll like that one. She's *bound* to like that one!" he'd say.

Now I'm holding the one I hope she'll like. It's beautiful, and simple, because Catherine is simple—in the largest, finest way. Not like me. I envy people like her, who are so sure of what they want. I stare at the ring, and think: *Even though taking this leap isn't something I'm certain I want to do, it's something she wants to do, and it's something I can do for her, as a way of giving to her, a way of loving her.*

My cell phone goes off, and as soon as I hear her say my name, I know. I'll never get to a place where I don't believe I somehow made it happen, simply by uttering the words. I listen, and tell her I love her, and envision myself wrapping my arms around her, letting her cry into my chest.

"I'll be on the first plane out in the morning," I say, and we discuss whether she should go to the hospital now, or wait, and go to the doctor tomorrow with me. The bleeding has stopped, and she's not in any pain, so we decide the best thing to do is to try to get some sleep.

"Maybe this one just wasn't meant to be," she says.

After we hang up, I go to the unit by the window and shut off the air-conditioning. Immediately the white noise vanishes. If Catherine had been here with me, she'd have done this as soon as we set down our suitcases. Holy quiet, she calls it.

I'm still holding the box, and I think: *Fate no longer has me hostage. The choice is mine. I have the power to make the woman I love immeasurably happy. Or I can stick with the status quo.* I'd like to say the decision was difficult, but I can't. I feel nothing so much as released, relieved. And I tell myself that since Catherine never knew I bought the ring, I'm not hurting her by returning it.

The next morning, when I buzz Zeb's room, there's no answer. No answer in Deb's room, either. When I go to the front desk to put their tabs on my credit card, I'm told Zeb has checked out, but left a note. *Nose broken. Will forward bill for rhinoplasty.* On my way back to the elevator, I spot Deb in the lobby.

"What happened?" I say.

"Twenty years of frustration," she says. "Balled into one fist."

"You hit him?"

"Don't be ridiculous. I think *he* wanted to hit *me*. But he never hurt me like that, you know? So instead he decked some asshole at the bar who'd been razzing me all night, and the guy up and smashed him. It was as if he was defending my honor or something. It was kind of sweet."

"The two of you saved my life," I say. "If anyone deserved to be punched in the face, it was me."

"It may happen yet," she says, and kisses me on the cheek. A liveried valet arrives and takes one of her bags in each hand. "Give Catherine my love," she says.

I'm not sure what the protocol is for redeeming a pledge, but I'm hoping it doesn't take long, because I have a plane to catch. As I step through the jingle-bell door, the owner of the pawnshop lifts his eyes from a thick paperback and dips his head in recognition. I finger the black velvet box in the pocket of my Windbreaker. The old man in the tweed jacket is gone.

"What happened to our friend?" I say.

"Moseyed on home."

"Did he find what he was looking for?"

"No." This answer, and the finality with which he delivers it, surprises me.

"How can you be so sure?"

"Percy wants to sell his insulin to buy a canoe. Comes in every week."

"Oh," I say, and find my inner O. Henry wondering if the man who sold his canoe needed the money to buy insulin. I feel bad for old Percy now, and wish he were here, although it's probably better time-wise that he's not.

I put the box on the counter. A speck of amusement crosses the owner's face.

"She said no?"

"Cold feet," I say, glancing down. "I'd like to trade back for the sax, if that's all right."

Without hesitating, the owner reaches under the counter and comes up with the case.

"You weren't going to try to sell it?" I say.

"My stepson's graduating from Hillsboro next week. I was planning to give it to him as a graduation present."

I hadn't considered that my failure of will might tamper with more lives than just mine and Catherine's, might muck up the universe in that way you hear about, where one missed bus changes the fate of millions.

"Is he really good?" I say.

"He doesn't play. I thought something like this might inspire him to start." Ah. Well. I'm all for the voodoo of the right instrument, but this golden fish would be wasted on a beginner.

"*C'est la vie,*" the owner says. He opens the box, unfastens the ring from its nest, and sticks a jeweler's loupe in his eye socket.

"You seem to have the right attitude," I say.

"Wanting things too much is a form of sadness," he says.

I examine the underside of the box. "Where'd this ring come from, anyway?"

He pauses, and in that pause I understand two things: The man doesn't lie, and he wouldn't be answering this question if I weren't already returning the ring.

"A newlywed came in," he says. "Her husband died on their honeymoon, and she needed the money to fly his body home to the U.S."

I step back from the counter. "That's the saddest thing I've ever heard," I say.

The owner shrugs. "Give yourself more time."

I feel sorry for him then, and am glad I'll soon be able to leave this place and its forlorn trinkets behind. I apologize, and explain I have a plane to catch. Then I thank him, saying I hope his stepson has a happy graduation and a nice life. He nods, shakes my hand, and stands there as I leave, lanky and dispassionate. On my way out, I ask him how he does it, working in a place where dreams come to an end.

"I think of it as a place where new dreams begin," he says.

I make it to Nashville International with just minutes to spare, and can't believe my luck when security doesn't pull me aside to search my sax case, the way they did on my way out. As I reach Gate B5, I break into the full sprint I haven't had occasion to use since my high school track days. The plane's air-conditioning hasn't kicked in yet, and I'm lightheaded and breathing heavily when we start down the tarmac. All I know is that leaving the ring behind feels like the right thing to do. As does flying home to Catherine. In fact, as we gain altitude and the air-conditioning comes on and we break through the clouds, slipping the surly bonds of Earth, all I can think about is the sight of her face.

# DOUBLE-BLIND

Saepe ne utile quidem est scire quid futurum sit.

*Often it is not even advantageous to know
what will be.* —Cicero

The day we chose to meet happened to fall on Avery's birthday; perhaps that added to my nervousness. For the first few years after my sister's death, I wouldn't do anything on her birthday. I suppose it was some form of adolescent protest. I let the phone ring, didn't show up to school or work, didn't turn on the computer. Some years, I didn't eat. But after a while it started to feel pointless, and I dropped the hollow exercise. Avery didn't much care what I did when she was alive; why would she care now that she was dead? Still, the date didn't escape my notice, and I wasn't surprised to find its iambic rhythm pulsing through my head as I traveled the walkway, climbed the steps, and pressed Ben's buzzer. November twenty-first.

A bleary-eyed, heavyset redhead answered the door, holding a piece of chalk. I pretended not to notice the enormous sweat marks extending like moist continents from both armpits. He took one look at me and said: "First of all, let's talk about the subatomic world."

This was a blind date—"double-blind," Ben had joked on the phone, when he'd heard I was working as a clinical epidemiologist on my way to a degree in psychology. We were both from the suburbs of Boston, both grad students, and both on shoestring budgets. I'd met his roommate Wolfgang at a costume party at the Design School three weeks earlier and had agreed to let him set me up. I was dressed in black from neck to boots and had pinned bras, socks, underpants, and dryer sheets all over myself. Wolf liked my costume—not the concept so much as the bras. Now the date was turning out exactly the way my mother would have predicted, an object lesson about what happens when a girl leaves the house wearing not only her heart but her panties on her sleeve.

I tried to act natural and offered my hand. It was then that I overheard a voice from inside the house: "That's why you don't give Franco the chalk! You'll never get it back!" Relieved, I realized this was the voice I knew from the phone. Following the voice came a man wearing a shirt with a quote from Nietzsche on it. His hair looked as if it had been styled in a wind chamber, and he was holding a lone chopstick.

"May we help you?" he said.

"Kim," I said. When this still appeared not to register,

I added, "We said Thursday the twenty-first, right? You're friends with Wolf?"

"*Right,*" he said, and quickly glanced from me to Franco, then back to me again.

"Does this mean you didn't bring the egg rolls?" Franco said, examining his chalk. Ben seemed torn, as if trying to choose from among several bad alternatives.

"Would you like to come in?" he said finally, prompting an expression of shock from Franco.

"Now?" Franco said. I could have invented a spontaneous migraine, or a sudden bout of narcolepsy, and perhaps I should have. But there was something about Ben that made me want to stay. He had one of those open, inquisitive faces most often seen on babies.

Franco yanked him aside, and with a ridiculous flourish of clandestine urgency, the two held a private pow-wow three feet away from me. I checked the door lintels for hidden cameras, figuring I must have been on one of those prank TV shows. Girl shows up for blind date. Date pretends to have forgotten and wants to let her in, but prop bystander protests: *Now? During the opening rites to dungeon bondage role-play?*

As it turned out, it was just like one of those shows, only much, much worse. Ben led me into a room full of strangers, an extremely hot room. Everyone in it was expecting Chinese food, and I didn't have any. I had a bag of Twizzlers in my purse, but I knew it wouldn't suffice; the very air in the room felt possessed of appetite. People were sprawled out everywhere: on the floor, on a Naugahyde couch, and in beanbag chairs. They all looked as if they'd either just woken up or had been drinking since noon. In

the center of the room was a two-sided chalkboard, completely covered with drawings and quotations. At first
I thought I'd walked in on some sort of Olympic-level
game of Pictionary. What I didn't know then was that it
was a free-form interdisciplinary brainstorming session,
or FIBS, and that it happened the third Thursday of every
month.

The point of the exercise, as it was explained to me,
was simple: All the participants were expected to share
something interesting about themselves or their field, and
whoever's contribution was deemed the most indispens-
able to life on the planet that night didn't have to pay
for his or her share of the takeout. Ben seemed vaguely
apologetic as he explained all of this, as if he expected I
might laugh myself into an epileptic fit at any moment,
and kept taking in my reactions with earnest, searching
eyes. But from the standpoint of a dissertation-writing
psychology student, it was oddly intriguing, and I was
already playing with such phrases as "Jungian impulse"
and "tribal mind."

"This is Kim," he told the group, with one hand at
my lower back as if I were a specimen. I gave a brief
wave from the wrist, à la Miss Massachusetts. I expected
that what would happen next would be people would
go around the room introducing themselves, and I might
be offered a glass of wine or maybe a cracker. Instead,
Franco produced a blindfold.

"What's that?"

"What's it look like?"

"An off-duty dust rag. What's it for?"

"You're uninitiated. We have to initiate you," he said.

I looked to Ben for reassurance, and he gave me a nod, the way a lion might nod at an antelope.

Franco began securing the bandana around my eyes. It was opaque and smelled like pipe tobacco.

"This seems a little creepy," I said.

"It's just a silly ritual," said a woman's voice. "We all had to do it." The words had the ersatz reassurance of a dentist calmly describing what he's about to do to your teeth.

"If there's going to be a sacrificial offering, I don't mind telling you, I'm not a virgin," I said. Nobody laughed, except for Franco, who guffawed wildly, which was worse than no one laughing. I wondered if my armpits were on their way to looking like his, then I realized I wasn't actually scared. The room had the odd comfort some great libraries have; it was hot, and populated with strangers, but safe-feeling.

Which was good, because now someone had taken me by the shoulders and was turning me in a circle. When he was done, he let go of me and spoke.

"The goal is to discover things that sound impossible when you first hear them but seem self-evident when you're finished," he said.

A moment later, it was someone else's turn to grab me by the shoulders and play spin-and-speak.

"Failure is not the enemy," he said. "Even the wrong choices can lead you in the right direction."

The next to approach was a woman; I could smell a hint of gingery perfume.

"When dreams come true, they often don't look like you thought they would. Be prepared for that." Was this meant to suggest that my dreams were going to come true tonight? If so, things were going to have to take some drastic turns mighty quickly.

"Those who are given great gifts are also given great obstacles."

"Wherever you are is the entry point."

"Use your intuition. There aren't many things that aren't best done intuitively." I wasn't sure suspension bridges were best built intuitively, but I held my tongue.

"The greatest truths are those whose opposite is also true." This from a man whose voice sounded a lot like Ben's. I considered an investigatory pawing of his face, but before I could act, it was someone else's turn.

This went on for about twenty minutes, each person in the group standing up, rotating me, then telling me something the likes of which you might expect to see on the bumper sticker of a flying car. I don't know if they had these things written out on index cards, or what. All I knew was that if they asked me to take the special pink drink, I wasn't drinking.

Finally: "Don't be constrained by past thinking or seemingly immutable laws. Remember the flight of the bumblebee."

"According to the laws of physics, bumblebees can't fly!" someone—probably not a physicist—blurted out. I'd had enough. I was thirsty, I was hot, I was tired of wearing some grad student's do-rag around my head. I'd heard of bad first dates, but this was a whole new universe of unexplored badness.

"Exactly what law of physics does the flight of the bumblebee contravene?" I said.

An indecipherable murmur moved through the room. "We'll get to your questions in a moment," said a deep, resonant voice. The cinematic portion of my brain pictured James Earl Jones sitting on a stool in the corner with a steaming cup of tea. "But first: Is there anything you wish to add to the collective knowledge of the group?"

The room went silent. I hesitated, but I didn't panic. I knew how to play games like this. My entire life was a game like this.

"A pigeon's feathers are heavier than its bones," I said. A risky bit of wisdom, and one I'd picked up from the alcoholic vagabond who haunted the Au Bon Pain in Harvard Square, true. But it seemed the sort of nugget this crowd could take to the bank. The next thing I knew, a sinewy, pungent mathematician was untying me. The first thing I saw was his shirt, which was covered with rows and rows of pi:

$$3.1415926$$
$$535897932$$
$$384626433$$
$$832795028$$
$$841971693$$
$$993751058$$
$$209749445$$

"You're in," he said.

"That was weird," I said. Ben and I were at the Middle East, a late-night coffeehouse in Central Square, where he'd just ordered an Irish coffee, a drink I've always considered to be a waste of all three ingredients.

He cocked his head.

"What?" I said.

"Nothing. It's just that I've made a conscious decision not to use the word *weird* anymore."

"That's weird," I said. "And this is because . . ."

"Everything is weird. Quantum superposition is weird. Electromagnetism is weird. Supersymmetric flip is weird. My parents have a friend who's allergic to snow. My neighbor is convinced that the Earth's weather patterns were fine until we punctured the atmosphere by flying into outer space."

"Your neighbor may win the Nobel Prize some day," I said, and took a sip of my hot chocolate. Ben's face brightened.

"My landlady," he said, "is convinced I'm stealing the fresh lightbulbs she puts in the hallway lamps and replacing them with my old ones."

"And are you?"

"I hadn't thought of it until Zarafinka suggested it! Now, if I ever need a plan to get rich sixty-five cents at a time, I've got one."

I found myself scanning my brain for examples of bizarre behavior, eager to match his tales. "I knew a cartoonist who used to unplug all of his appliances at night, to save on his electric bill," I said.

Ben stirred his coffee. "We should fix him up with my landlady. They could make frugal cartoons together."

"We *should*," I said. "My sister once set two people

up, and then every year, on Valentine's Day, they would send a card to *her*."

Ben hesitated, and I could tell he was debating whether to comment on our own situation. We were, after all, on an arranged date ourselves.

"Of course, if it all went south, she could have gotten hate mail every year," I said. "You never know with these things." Ben's eyes flashed. "I'm sorry, did that sound cynical?" I said. "That probably sounded cynical."

"It sounded honest," he said, leaning back. "I like honest." His expression made me both happy and nervous. Usually I didn't tell stories involving my sister—it was impossible to mention her without running the risk of having to say what happened to her—and I wondered why I had broken my own rule for him.

"I once went on a date with a guy who could recite *Hamlet* backwards," I said, to bring us back to weirdnesses.

Ben set down his mug. "Telmah," he said.

"Not a very marketable skill."

"Wolf claims he used to go out with the boomerang champion of the world," he said. "Back in Germany. I've seen a photograph. Picture Wolf with a seven-foot-tall Amazon." I imagined Wolf with his palms pinned by a Teutonic huntress wearing nothing but a boomerang, and almost laughed.

"What do you call a boomerang that doesn't work?" I said. Ben waited. "A stick!" I said, slapping the table. I think this is incredibly funny, even though no one else ever does. Ben smiled, charitably, and I decided I liked him;

there was a genuine warmth about him. I hadn't been on a date since the guy at the dry cleaners asked me out while paying for his shirts, then took me to a whodunit dinner theater. Ben seemed full of potential: brainy, attractive, entertaining. My own young Richard Feynman.

"What's the weirdest thing that's ever happened to you?" he said, drawing his chair in closer.

"I thought you didn't use that word," I said. Under the table I nudged his foot, to show I meant it in a friendly way.

"What occurrence is the most standard deviations away from your normal range of experience?" he said.

If he hadn't asked, I'd have been able to cover the tablecloth with my list. But of course in that moment, I couldn't think of a single abnormal thing. I stared at the menu, as if the words *baba ghanoush* were memory's shibboleth. The only thing that came to mind, bizarrely enough, was a third-grade paper titled "The Miraculus Miracle" that had been unearthed recently when my parents' basement flooded.

"I've never gotten over the sheer improbability that I was born," I said.

Ben's chin was resting on his hands. "I'm afraid that won't do," he said.

I glanced about the restaurant. By the front window, two men were playing klezmer music, one on the clarinet and the other on an accordion. All the tables had little tea lights on them and most were occupied by couples or small groups. Toward the back, a Sephardic-looking woman sat at a table draped in black velvet; in front of her was a crystal ball and a sign that said READINGS BY RENATA.

"I once had my palm read, in Venice, and the woman said: 'You're going to be famous, but not in the way you think.' Does that count?"

"What do you think she meant?"

"I have no idea. That's what makes it weird," I said. I gestured in the direction of Renata. "Do you think she got her crystal ball off the Internet?"

"Do you think you're going to be famous?"

"I hope not. I feel bad for famous people. They can never enjoy their falafels in peace."

"Fame as inconvenience," he said.

"You think it's easy being Eartha Kitt?"

"Eartha Kitt is dead."

"Exactly. First you're famous, then you're dead. What good does it do you?"

The third-grade paper that survived the flood was about a girl who loved so strongly, she could bring things back to life. First a butterfly. Then the family dog. Then the man who gave her Budweiser stickers who always went jogging on her street. But when the newspapers found out about her power and broadcast it, she lost it, and was unable to bring back the thing she loved most of all.

"Here's something weird," I said. "I know a guy who dreamed he died and went to heaven, and at the pearly gates, Saint Peter asked if he had any regrets. He said: 'Yeah. I could have been a great accountant.' Before the dream, the idea of accounting had never entered his head.

After the dream, he took classes, got certified, and now crunches numbers for a loyal cadre of New Yorkers who swear by his expertise."

Ben poked my hand with his finger. "But that isn't something that happened to *you*," he said, pressing my skin as if it held an invisible buzzer. I'm sure his touchy-feely curiosity was intended to open me up and put me at ease, but it had the opposite effect, and I withdrew. It was disturbing to realize how much I wanted to impress him. I wasn't used to trying to impress people; that had always been Avery's domain. She'd been so good at it that I simply bowed out of the race, became the pensive little sister with her face in a crossword puzzle. Now here I was, cheeks flushed, lips laced with chocolate, scouring my life for odd events. And all I could think of was Avery.

"What's the weirdest thing that's ever happened to *you*?" I said, feeling ingenious. I always forget that it's possible to turn the tables.

"The strangest thing that's ever happened to me is still happening," Ben said in a low voice.

When I was twelve, I spent a summer learning how to raise one eyebrow—time that now felt wisely invested.

"Oh *really*," I said.

He took my hand. "Come downstairs," he said. Then he led me down the stairs and over to the men's room, where he tried to get me to go in with him. Never have I so rapidly amended my hopes for an evening.

"I don't think so," I said. "You seem nice and every-thing, but I'm good out here."

"I'll keep my pants zipped," he said, laughing. "I just want to show you something."

"That's what they all say."

"It'll only take a minute." I kept waiting for another patron to approach and find Ben grasping my hand, trying to coax me into the men's room. I wanted to hear how he'd explain himself.

"No way, Benjamin. Men's bathrooms are vile."

"We can use the ladies' room, then," he said, moving us two feet to the left.

"Why does it have to be a bathroom at all?"

"I just need somewhere dark. Trust me."

"I used to trust you, until you started acting synaptically impaired," I said. "Although I suppose you've seemed a little insane from the start."

He dropped my hand. "Do you really think that?" he said. His face grew serious. "Either you trust me, or you don't."

My mother claims that people show you everything you need to know about them within the first hour of meeting them, it's just that most of us aren't paying attention. And I have to say, she might be right. If I look closely enough, all the chords of our four years together were struck that first night: Ben's eccentricity, his warmth, his need for me to prove my love. As were my desire to please him, my skepticism, my ultimate inability to see things the way he did. All the notes of our undoing were there, alongside the notes of our joy.

"Fine," I said. "But this had better be quick."

We stepped inside and Ben closed the door. It was completely dark. The bathroom thankfully had one of those auto-spritz air fresheners that are used to mask all manner of odiousness.

"Now, just bear with me," he said. "I know this is going to seem strange." He did something. "There. Do you see that?"

"See what?"

"Hold on. Maybe there needs to be a little light." He opened the door a crack. "Now can you see them?"

I watched him slowly rippling the fingers of one hand. "Are you casting a spell?" I said. "If there's an albino rabbit in here, I don't see him."

"Now?"

"No."

"How about now?"

"This could easily become tiresome."

"You don't see very faint"—he paused, as if he hated to articulate what he was about to say—"rays of light coming off the ends of my fingertips?"

I laughed, and worried. "You're kidding, right? This is a joke?"

"I know it sounds insane. I mean, it sounds insane to me, too. I just needed to show someone." He was still wiggling his fingers and staring. "Maybe I'm imagining it?"

I tried again, first concentrating hard, then relaxing my focus. But I couldn't. I couldn't see a thing.

"Have you been playing games with plutonium?" I said.

"No," he said. He dug his hands in his pockets. "You think I'm crazy."

"No, I don't," I said. I meant it. I knew what it was like to have something you didn't usually tell people, and I appreciated that he was willing to share his freaky secret.

"'Nothing is to be feared,'" I said. "'It is only to be understood.' Although I guess I should have spun you in a circle first."

His face opened in a smile. "Marie Curie," he said.

"Now there was a chick with a high tolerance for weirdness."

"I like her style," he said. He lifted the back of my hand and kissed it. "I like yours, too."

"You are an odd one, mister," I said. "But it's possible I could learn to like you anyway." I clapped my hands together. "Can we get out of here?"

The temperature had dropped considerably, and driving home, we ran the heat full blast. We talked about our work, our roommates, our favorite foods (his: pasta puttanesca; mine: watermelon). In the end, I didn't tell him about Avery. Not that night anyway. I just said "my sister," casually, breezily, the way anyone would. I didn't tell him that she may have been in a hurry to get home—that it had been her birthday. That it was theorized she must have assumed, after waiting several seconds after the first train had passed, that the crossing arm was malfunctioning. That she must not have realized, as she drove around it, that it was still down because another train was coming.

I was eight years old at the time—third grade—and when they told me what had happened, I didn't understand. *Another train was coming.* It sounded like the punch line to a joke. I kept waiting for everyone to laugh, and my sister to jump out from behind the couch and eat her cake—mint chocolate chip ice cream, my favorite. When they asked her what kind she wanted that year, she said she was on a diet; I knew she'd requested mint chocolate chip for me. But she never jumped out from behind the couch, and no one ever laughed, and at some point they must have thrown the cake away, because when I looked for it in the freezer on my own uncelebrated birthday, three months later, it was gone.

At every red light, I studied Ben's reflection in the windshield and wondered if when I dropped him off, he would kiss me. I shifted the car into park beside his mailbox. Then it came to me.

"The strangest thing that ever happened to me is that when I was eighteen, I received a letter from myself that I'd written when I was ten."

"In a dream?"

"In the mail."

"You've succeeded in collapsing the space-time continuum then?"

"Our camp counselor had us write them, and address them to our permanent residences. I couldn't believe it. To me, from myself, in an almost unrecognizable hand."

"What'd it say?"

"Dear Kim, How's it going? Do you still go to summer camp? Probably not. I have seven million mosquito bites, and Mom found Sabrina up a tree. But you must know that already. I guess there isn't anything I can tell you that you don't already know."

"That's sweet," he said. He was running his fingers through strands of my hair. I swiveled so I was facing him.

"You know, the choice thing would be to have that happen in reverse. I'd like to receive a letter from a self many years my senior. Maybe she'd have some wisdom to impart."

"You really think it'd make a difference?"

"Of course. She could warn me, give me advice: Watch out for that Ben character." I winked.

"And you'd listen?"

"Wouldn't you?"

"I'm not sure that even if given the gift of prophecy, I'd have the inclination or ability to do anything differently." We were both silent. "What's wrong?" he said. "You look sad."

"I'm not," I said quietly. He got out of the car and walked around his yard for a minute, then climbed back in. "For you," he said, handing me a small, delicately curved branch. He plucked a stray leaf from its base. "An off-duty boomerang."

I'm not a sentimental person, but do you know I still have that stick? It sits atop my mantel, alongside some river stones and pigeon feathers I picked up on vacation in New Mexico.

He put his hand on my shoulder. "Consider yourself warned," he said, returning my wink. Then he left and took the long gravel path to the house. When he reached the end, he hopped up the steps, turned around, and waved. It felt as if he were waving at me from across a great distance, an unbridgeable abyss—across all the distance between what has been and what is to come.

# THE FAR SIDE

# OF THE MOON

In those days, I had girlfriends the way some people have freckles. I wish I could recall them all individually, but I've retained only the more peculiar traits of each, resulting in an odd farrago that looms in my mind like a Picasso. There was the girl whose prep school roommate had advised her to put root beer ChapStick on her labia before oral sex, and another who had a parlor gag where she could sign her name with her foot. One girl's mother had been in and out of mental hospitals her whole life; I remember she once served us roasted chicken complete with burned feathers and cooked innards. I drove to Killington, Vermont, for a weekend with a lively girl-friend who met me at the door wearing nothing but a bra, panties, and ski boots. I'm pretty sure she was different from the one who used to whisper delicious things to me while we were in bed, but she was too shy to speak up about it, prompting me, at the tender age of twenty-two, to consider purchasing a hearing aid, as a kind of sex toy. The prettiest was a girl who belonged to a performance troupe called The Belly Dancers for Peace & Justice, who was convinced she'd seen the Virgin of Guadalupe etched on the hood of a '76 Monte Carlo.

There was one girl who stands out. Her name was Mandy Purcell. She was working at the swankiest old folks' home in Arlington, Massachusetts, when we met, during the summer of 1977. I was there doing community service as a result of my work with the Billboard Liberation Front ("adding the blemish of truth" was our motto); Mandy was there voluntarily. All the old guys loved her—the smooth young skin, the frank blue eyes, the gauzy hippie skirts. But there was one fogy, Harold, who reserved for her a special kind of affection. He had that condition old people sometimes get that's like a combination of Tourette's syndrome and Zen wisdom. Whenever Mandy would bring him orange juice or change the station on the TV set, he'd start.

"Want to hear a one-word description of the worst blow job I ever had?" Mandy would never answer, but he didn't need encouragement.

"*Fantastic,*" he said.

At other times, he was more philosophical: "Appearance only goes so far in life. You show me the most beautiful woman in the world, and I'll show you the guy who's tired of fucking her."

One day he told a joke I don't remember, except that the punch line had something to do with getting scrod in the pluperfect.

"Harold, my man, you are the court jester of the moribund," I said. "You must be the funniest septuagenarian I've ever met."

"I'm a sexagenarian," he said.

"You most certainly are."

In the kitchen, I tried to score points with Mandy.

"Seriously?" I said. "You're going to take that from him? What about women's lib? What about respect?"

Mandy stuck a plate sideways in a rack to dry. "Harold stormed the beach at Normandy," she said. "He gets to say whatever he wants."

She wouldn't go out with me. My community service ran through the month of June, and I think I asked her out every week. She always said no, but nicely, claiming she had some sort of boyfriend, although I never saw the guy. After my gig at the nursing home was up, I kind of forgot about her. Until the August afternoon when Ace showed up at my door with the car.

It was a Jaguar convertible. Ace had bought it at a police auction for no money. He'd found a pair of fuzzy handcuffs in the trunk, and dangling from the rearview mirror was an icon of the Evil Queen from *Snow White*. The Evil Queen had been his first erotic fixation, so he'd felt the car was speaking to him. Before taking it on its first joyride—first under new ownership—he came to get me.

We screamed up Route 2 with the top down. A car is not always the answer to the meaningless monotony of life. But sometimes it is. While we revved at the end of an exit ramp, blood thick with adrenaline, I experienced what I can only describe as divine inspiration. I took off my sunglasses.

"Let's go rescue Mandy," I said.

I loved Ace because he never said no to anything. He'd been my closest friend throughout college, where I was first drawn to him because of his mastery of the art of enjoyment. Ace had taken the SAT stoned and had still gotten a nearly perfect score. Freshman week, during which he was blitzed 98 percent of the time, he found a smoke shop on Mass. Ave. and got a tattoo of Chaucer on his left biceps. When he discovered that the local squirrels were not afraid to jump from the tree limb outside his fourth-floor window into his dorm room, he made a nest for them, fed them, and then on walks through Harvard Yard would use his Dr. Dolittle charms to impress women. Before he got kicked out, he'd been working on a thesis proposal to rewrite the Bible in the anapestic tetrameter of Dr. Seuss.

> *Who will cast the first stone? Who would like to begin?*
> *Who is ready to judge? Who has lived without sin?*
> *'Cause to love one another—I've told you before—*
> *You must love EVERY other, including this whore.*

When we got to the nursing home, it turned out Mandy didn't want to be rescued.

"I'm working," she said, eyeing the car skeptically. "Come back at seven."

By the time we went back we'd already split a six-pack of Schlitz in Ace's garage. Logistics had gotten away from us, and it was 7:45 when I rang the bell. Harold answered.

"She's gone," he said. "You blew it, Bub."

"Fuck," I said. Before I could elaborate, Mandy came walking up the street.

"I figured you weren't coming," she said. "I couldn't wait around all night."

"But you came back."

"I forgot something," she said, mounting the steps and slipping her narrow body between me and the door frame. In her wake I smelled patchouli.

*What'd you forget?* I wanted to ask, because I had the feeling she hadn't forgotten anything at all, but I didn't want to push things. I had already shown up forty-five minutes late for our first date.

While she was inside, Harold squeezed my shoulder. "Next time, bring me one of those beers you been drinking."

Once we were on our way, Ace kept checking Mandy out in the rearview mirror.

"Mitch tells me you're the flower of Golden Meadows," he said. Before I could protest, he added, "Not in so many words."

"Oh, really," Mandy said. "May I ask where we're going?"

"Don't you think you should have asked that before you got in the car?" Ace said. Half my time with Ace is spent on disaster control.

"To Cronin's," I said, twisting to face her. "It's a bar in Cambridge. If that's all right."

"Sure," said Mandy. "Why not."

"*Mandy, Candy,*" Ace said. While we were in his garage, he'd also smoked half a joint. "I like you already." He grinned. "Tell us something about yourself we would never guess."

The top was down and Mandy's hair was airborne; she kept pulling strands of it out of her mouth. "I used to work for a greeting card company," she said after thinking for a minute.

"And?" said Ace. "Did you get fired for embezzling truckloads of money?"

"I quit. I designed a card that said *Tikkun Olam,* and they didn't like that it was in Hebrew. They said: 'This is America. Write in English.'"

"What does it mean?" I said.

"'Repair the World.' It was translated on the inside."

"Bastards," said Ace.

"It's all right," Mandy said. "I didn't like it there that much anyway. I hardly ever got to design. Most of my time was spent using a glue gun and glitter. I worked with glitter so much that one day I sneezed and it came out sparkles."

"Awww," I said. "Like a fairy. A fairy with a head cold."

"Exactly," said Mandy.


At Cronin's, I ordered a pair of Buds and found us a booth in the back. On the way in, Ace had stopped to talk to some friends of his who were congregated outside with their Harleys. The song playing on the jukebox was barely audible above the noise, but I could make it out.

I said: "Tell me if I'm crazy, but—"

"You're crazy," Mandy said.

"Don't you think a better name for this album would have been *The Far Side of the Moon*? It's not the part that's in shadow that they're singing about. It's the hemisphere that's never visible from Earth, that's permanently remote."

"Why don't you write Roger Waters a letter," she said.

"I'm serious."

"So am I."

A couple walked in with their arms around each other and sat in a nearby booth.

"Your boyfriend doesn't mind you coming out like this?" I said.

Mandy brought her beer bottle to her lips. She had one of those sexy gaps between her two front teeth. "What do you care what my boyfriend thinks?" she said. "Word on you is you have a new girlfriend every week."

"Because the one girl I really want won't say yes."

She gave me one of her forthright glances, and I felt like a student whose paper was being graded in front of him, a patient whose X-rays were being examined.

"Maybe you like them that way," she said. "Permanently remote."

I laughed. "Even if that were true—and I'm not saying it is—can a man help what he likes?"

"I know all about your type," she said. I noticed with surprise that she was farther along with her beer than I was. "You won't believe me. But I do."

I reached for her hands. "Prove it to me," I said.

She held my gaze for several unblinking seconds, then let go. Her eyes migrated to a spot beyond my left shoulder.

"Your friend," she said. "Is he always like that?"

Ace was coming toward us, wearing one of the bikers' helmets. He put three more beers on the table and sat down.

"Ask me a question in Latin," he said. "And I will answer you in Greek."

"Is that how you greeted your friends with the hogs?" Mandy said.

"My greetings are audience-appropriate," Ace said. Years later, while Ace is giving a lecture titled "Don't Ever Pay for Electricity When You Can Make It Simple and Cheap at Home," a man in the crowd will raise his hand. "If you're so smart, how come you're not rich?" he'll ask. To which Ace will reply: "If you're so rich, how come you're not smart?" An audience-appropriate riposte, to be sure. But I also believe it marks the exact moment at which Ace became obsessed with making millions of dollars.

"Ace speaks five languages," I said. "He has one of the highest IQs on record."

Mandy turned to him. "Does that mean you're happy?"

"Be careful of this one," I said. "She'll see into your soul."

Ace rotated the bottles of beer in and out of a triangle pattern. "As my father used to say: 'There are two ways of being unhappy. Not getting what you want. And getting what you want.'" The overhead lights reflected in the hyaline surface of his helmet. "He also used to make us stick our pencils up our noses and leave them there for the rest of dinner if we were caught doing homework at the table."

Mandy sat back. "How could you eat with a pencil dangling in front of your mouth?"

"And he once put stickers on everything in my bedroom, indicating how much it had cost. The bed frame, the lamps, the desk, the pillowcases, the carpet. All with price tags on them."

Ace had been my best friend for five years, and I'd never heard any of this. I didn't even know he *had* a father.

"Don't take this the wrong way," I said, "but are you full of shit right now?"

Apparently Mandy believed him. "Ace is always full of shit," she said. "*Except* for now."

After that, no one said anything. I guess Ace didn't know how to live up to the burden of not being full of shit, and I didn't know what to say. Eventually Mandy turned to me.

"What about your father?" she said.

"If you find him," I said, "tell him I say hi."


I can't recall who drove, or how we even made it to the Little League field in one piece. All I remember is lying with my back flat on a wet sea of grass, with Ace on my left somewhere and Mandy over on my right. And all those stars.

"*Ad astra per aspera,*" I said.

"Okey dokey, Sir Polyglot," said Mandy.

"It's part of our message," I said. "To the aliens."

*Voyager 2* had been launched the weekend before, carrying a Golden Record with sounds from our planet. Among them were footsteps, heartbeat, laughter, ocean surf, birdsong, frogs, a ship's horn, a kiss, and this phrase. They'd also included a diverse selection of music, from a Brandenburg concerto to "Johnny B. Goode." Ace and I had slept through the original broadcast of the launch, but had watched the *Saturday Night Live* coverage later. Father Guido Sarducci announced that the first communication from extraterrestrials was being received. Once decoded, the message said: "Send more Chuck Berry."

"*Ad astra per* what?" Mandy said.

"It means 'Through hardships to the stars,'" I said. "They put it on the Golden Record. But first they translated it into Morse code."

"Of course they did," Mandy said.

"No aliens will ever intercept that thing," Ace said. "It'll just be a weird gift to ourselves. In the future."

"That's so typical," Mandy said. "We always want to fill the void. We don't know how to just be still and listen."

We stared at the stars for a few minutes. Then, out of nowhere, Mandy groaned. "Is the planet spinning right now, or is it just me?"

"Ho, baby," I said. "Are you okay?"

"Maybe you should lie down," Ace said.

Mandy groaned in a higher frequency.

"Here," I said, reaching out. "Hold my hand." She took my hand and squeezed it, hard.

"What about me?" Ace said. So I stuck out my other arm and held his hand, too. I imagined how the three of us must have looked from outer space, strung together like paper dolls.

"I'm cold," Mandy said.

"Come here," I said. She crawled over and laid her head on my chest. I let go of Ace and smoothed Mandy's hair with my hand. I loved the weight of her head and the scent of her hair. I felt ridiculously happy.

"Mandy, I know we're both wasted right now. Plus

we've got this yahoo with us. So I won't ask you to marry me. But one day, someday, will you let me take you out on a proper date? One date, anywhere you want?"

I waited. I wished a shooting star would streak through the sky like a rocket.

"Yes," she said.

I had anticipated evenings before, but this was an anticipation of epic proportions. When Saturday night finally rolled around, I decided to buy her flowers, just to shake things up a bit, throw a curve ball at her sense that she had my number. I'd never bought a woman flowers and I had no idea what to get. After a stupidly long time at the florist, I decided on peonies. I liked the way they looked overstuffed; I figured I was getting more bang for my buck.

On the way to Golden Meadows, I passed one of those churches with an outdoor sign whose message changes every week. They'd just put up a new one: EVEN JESUS HAS A FISH STORY.

When Harold answered the door, he took one look at my bouquet and began to shake his head. "There's no fool like a young fool," he said.

"What are you, the receptionist?" I said. "Why do you keep answering the door?"

Mandy came down the stairs in a short yellow dress. She looked better than gorgeous; she looked out of this world. She walked right up to me, wearing an expression of barely contained delight. Whatever it was she had to say, it was going to be good.

"I got into art school," she said. "I'm going to Rome!"

There are some moments in life that are so disorienting, so surreal, you find yourself saying the exact opposite of what you feel.

"That's so wonderful," I said. If she'd been smiling any wider, her mouth would have jumped off her face.

"I didn't tell anyone I was applying," she said. "Not even my parents. I never thought I'd get in. They only take about four students a year. I just found out today."

"That's wonderful," I said again. I'm convinced I was in shock; I'm lucky she didn't ask me who the President was. "We'll have to make a toast."

A shadow crossed her face. "You don't understand," she said. "I can't go out with you now. There's too much I need to do before I leave."

"You *can't* go out with me now, or you don't *want* to go out with me now?"

"Don't be like that," she said. Then she ran into the living room and came back holding a wooden cigar box. "I have something for you," she said. "But it's for the future. You can't open it until"—she paused—"Twenty-ten." *Twenty-ten*. The word sounded absurd and impossible, an abstraction out of science fiction.

The box's lid had been engraved with a dove with both wings spread open. "Did you make this?" I said.

She nodded. "Just give it a good bang against a rock and it'll open," she said. "It's only sealed with Elmer's."

I set the box down and put my hands on the bony wings of her hips. "Why don't you give it to me in person?"

"Take it now," she said. "But don't open it until twenty-ten." She pinched me. "Promise."

"I promise," I said. A moment passed, then Harold's

voice came from the TV room. "For the love of God, kiss her already!"

She sent me postcards, mostly decorated with her drawings, but a few had words thrown in, in a snaking pattern around the border, or inside the petals of a flower. I thought about her every day, but for some reason I could never bring myself to write her back. I suppose I felt abandoned, plus she was just so far away. The box remained sealed. I was a man of principles—principles that were circumscribed by boundaries of my own invention, but principles nonetheless.

For a few years, I worked as a DJ on Boylston Street, until I got tired of wearing earplugs every night. While I lived in Providence, I was a research assistant to a professor who used me more to coordinate his travel plans than to do any actual research. I had a brief stint as a cub reporter until everyone at the newspaper lost their jobs. I worked in sales, where the better I became at it, the more I hated it. I got in on the ground floor of a video start-up that tried unsuccessfully to create demand for virtual tours of college campuses. I even had a job at an aerospace company, where I once carried a rocket nosecone on my shoulder. I've been a music tutor, a limo driver, a service technician, and a short-order cook. All told, I've lived in thirteen cities over the past thirty-three years. I was married once, when I lived in San Antonio, but it didn't take; I probably shouldn't have let myself be talked into it in the first place. People speak of not being able to outrun their ghosts, but for me it was just the opposite. I always felt as if I couldn't quite catch up to mine.

For the past couple of years, I've worked as a sound engineer for the film industry. I'll let you in on a little trick of the trade: The best way to portray silence in a movie is not with an absence of noise, but with the merest, tiniest sound.

Ace made his fortune patenting a microchip with the Bible on it—the non-Seussian version—that people could wear as jewelry. He now lives four hours north of me, in Big Sur, in a house with one wall made entirely of glass.

I haven't heard Mandy Purcell's name since that summer, so if she got anywhere with her art, she didn't go platinum with it. I've searched for her on the Internet, but with no luck. I realize she could be dead. I used to dream that she flew across the ocean for me, in the form of a huge white bird. It's funny—she and Harold were both in love with the song "Can't Take My Eyes Off You" by Frankie Valli and the Four Seasons; it played constantly at the nursing home. The song opens with a long major third, so now I think of Mandy whenever I'm stuck in traffic on the 10. The major third is the interval to which most car horns are tuned.

It's a Thursday night in Culver City. The year is 2010. *Voyager 2* is in the constellation known as Telescopium; it has traveled more than eight billion miles. I don't know where along the way I lost the box. But I've started dreaming of Mandy again. In the dream, I find her. She's alive, but her last name has changed. She asks me to give her one reason why she should go out with me. I tell her that I was a fool, that all twenty-two-year-olds are fools, that it's a law of nature. Plus, she owes me a date. She's the kind of person who believes in second chances, and she's willing to give me one. On one condition: I have to tell her what was in the box. I have the dream over and over, and my answer is always different. The box was filled with white feathers. With painted rocks. With starlight. With poems, the most beautiful poems, that were all unbelievable, and all true. The box contained a list of everything I wish I had never done, and I tear it up and toss it into the sea. The box contained a list of everything I still wish I could do.

In one version, I confess that I lost it. That my intentions were good, but that somehow, in the execution, I screwed up royally. That this is, in fact, the story of my life. Mandy tells me that she understands, she always understood, she knew this about me, and she forgives me.

This morning, a friend forwarded me something that's making the rounds. It's a list of "Better Names" for record albums. Most of them are jokey, but there's one that takes itself seriously: *The Far Side of the Moon*. I think I know who wrote it. I'm going to track her down. And if she asks me her question, I'm ready. The box, I'll say, was empty.

## SOMEDAY IS TODAY

My sister's husband died recently, and sorrow has made her a little girl again. Although she's thirty-nine, I keep catching glimpses of her little-girl face, the face I know from old photographs and junior high yearbooks. She's lost weight, and that adds to the impression, contributes to this parade of unbidden memories from when we were kids growing up outside Boston. She was the bony brunette sister, the reader in the family, very pretty, with high cheekbones and a blunt way with words. I was the oldest, blond, the people-pleaser.

I'm visiting her in California, trying to help out with the kids. There are three girls: fraternal twins who are six, and another girl who's four. When her husband died, my sister took her children to a field of daffodils a few blocks from their house, spread out a blanket, and had them sit down. The sun was high and bright; their father had died the day before. When she told them, the outgoing twin said: "How soon do we get a new daddy?"; the shy one said: "I knew it"; and the youngest asked if she could go play on the tire swing.

The house my sister lives in was undergoing major renovations when her husband died, so she and I and the kids are all crammed into the casita, a small abode in the back, beside the pool. The main house is stately, elegant— tragic. The perfect setting for something heartbreaking to happen—how could we not have seen it before? It looks like an old plantation house, with white columns and a second-story balcony. The workmen have cleared out all the rooms; there's a plastic tarp over the piano, and dust everywhere. Dust coats the soles of your feet when you leave.

My sister has found some comfort in the widow boards on the Internet. One of them has a list of Ten Helpful Hints for Getting Through This Most Difficult Time in Your Life. Hint Number 7: Learn to Expect the Unexpected. "Expect to cry at odd times: At the sight of a couple holding hands, at the sound of the doorbell ringing." The bit about the doorbell got to me. As if, some- where in your psyche, some part of you thinks he's come home—and then remembers. My sister doesn't wait for the doorbell. After the girls are asleep, she walks the stone path to the empty house, lies down on the floor of what used to be her master bedroom, and wails. I hear her. I don't join her; I don't know how to join her. When the doctor delivered the final news, I put my hand against her back. "Don't touch me," she said quietly.

The pair of tulip trees outside the casita are in bloom. I've never seen them blooming before; I must never have been here at this time of year. It's not that my sister and

I are not close, but we live on opposite coasts. I usually come to visit only at holidays. Lately my sense of humor has taken a sardonic, self-deprecating turn, and when I first heard about the widow board's advice, I nearly said: Expect the sister, the one you had almost given up on, to come for a visit and actually stay for a while.

I take the girls to the House of Pancakes so my sister can sleep in. She's exhausted, and the Lexapro makes it worse. I don't have any children of my own, so my mothering skills are a little ad hoc. I know there are lines that need to be drawn, I just never seem to know where to draw them. At the House of Pancakes, there are no chopsticks—a blessing. At the Chinese restaurant last week, the waiter gave the girls chopsticks made of hardened plastic, then acted surprised when they used them like drumsticks against their plates and started mock-stabbing one another. The way I see it, give a six-year-old a chopstick at your own peril. I know that elsewhere on the planet there are girls their age who have already been using chopsticks skillfully for years. With blond hair and blue eyes, these girls couldn't look less Asian. They don't even look like my sister. They look as if they were born to me.

We're sitting at a booth just inside the revolving door. The four-year-old is in a booster seat she doesn't need, but I'm letting her use it anyway. They are coloring in farm scenes with nubs of crayons.

"Tell us the story again," says the outgoing twin. During the car ride over, she has asked that we call her Coco.

"Which one?" I say.

Coco rolls her eyes. "About the chicken," she says. The shy twin slides her paper place mat away from her, but still holds her flesh-colored crayon. The youngest one continues drawing.

"Your father was doing orientation for his new consulting job," I say.

"What's the O word mean again?" Coco asks.

"When they make you do things to fit in with the group."

The shy twin tilts her head. "What's the other O word?"

"What other O word?"

"The one you taught us before? About God knowing everything?"

"*Omniscient,*" I say, and the girls grin. "So. Your father was at orientation, and there was a scavenger hunt. The assignment they gave his team was to find the freshest meat in Chinatown. And your daddy, because he was so smart, figured out a surefire way to win." The girls start giggling. They know what's coming. "The next morning, he showed up at company headquarters, with a live chicken on a leash!"

When the waiter arrives, I let them order whatever they want—stacks of pancakes topped with whipped cream and blueberry sauce, piles of hash browns, sausage patties for everyone. I have my sister's credit card in my purse. It has her husband's name on it. When you call the house, you still hear her husband's voice on the machine.

The waiter's a lefty, and his wrist bends at an acute angle when he writes.

"My name is Coco," says my niece.

"Pan-cakes for Co-co," the waiter says, sweetly.

After he's gone, the shy twin scoots back into a corner of the booth. "I want to be Saltine Teacup," she says.

"Why, *Saltine Teacup*. What a pretty name," I say.

The youngest one stops drawing. "I'm Pepper."

I slide forward with my elbows on the table. "Did you know that Pepper was the name of a Dalmatian my mommy and daddy had when they were first married?" The girls shake their heads: They did not know. "I have a picture of them standing in front of a cottage by a lake, with the Dalmatian in front. My mother's wearing a white bikini with black polka dots. Can you girls guess why?"

"To go swimming?" Pepper says.

"To match the dog!" I say. Coco wrinkles her nose, and we laugh. After a pause, they all start coloring again. Saltine Teacup looks up from her place mat. Superimposed on the chest of the farmer in the picture, she has drawn an enormous red heart.

"Our daddy's with your daddy now," she says.

I wipe a smudge from her cheek with my napkin. "That's right," I say.


When we get home, I let the girls tell me what to do. First we bounce around on the trampoline, then I push them on the swings, then we ride in the Barbie cars, circling the pool. I'm amazed at the stamina my sister has secretly had all these years. When they ask if we can jump on the trampoline again, I suggest we play a game called Auntie Takes a Nap. I lie down on the bounce mat and close my eyes. Coco laughs and punches me in the chest.

"Ow!" I say. It hurt more than it should have. "Please

don't do that." I pull up my shirt—I'm not wearing a bra—and dip my chin, examining myself. There's a large purple bruise that covers my right breast. My niece's eyes grow wide with horror, then she starts to cry.

"It's okay, sweetie," I say. I slide my shirt down, sit up, and rub her arm. "You didn't do that. It was like that already." Before I flew out, I had to have a breast cyst aspirated. It was unlike anything I've ever experienced—the hypnotically thin needle, the oddly cheerful banter, the eerie amber fluid filling the reservoir. Had the doctor given me laughing gas? It felt as though he had, although I couldn't quite remember. I remember telling him about my brother-in-law.

"One weekend he was skiing with his children, and a month later, he was dead," I said.

"And they don't know how he contracted it?"

"No. Doesn't staph live on our bodies all the time?"

"Yes, but . . . How'd it get into his blood?"

"Nobody knows," I said. "Maybe the dentist? Or a puncture wound?" I looked at the needle, then at him, then we both became silent. He used the ultrasound on me when he was finished. Then he gave me an ice pack to stick in my bra and told me to cut down on my caffeine intake.

"Is that what causes cysts?"

"We don't really know what causes them," he said. The body and its independent desires. A number of my childless friends had begun developing uterine fibroids in the past couple of years. It was as if our wombs were saying: *We don't need you! We can make things all by ourselves!*

. . .

After supper the girls change into their pajamas and brush their teeth, and we all pile into the one big bed that's actually three twin-size beds squished together. Instead of reading to them from a book, they like it when I make up a story based on an old photograph. They especially like the photos where their mom and I are as young as they are now. I've brought a stack with me in my duffel bag.

"Who's that?" they say.

"That's me!"

"What's wrong with your hair?"

"We had something called perms. It was your mommy's idea. We did them at home, and they smelled bad when we went swimming."

Coco props her head on one elbow. "How bad?"

"They smelled like rotten fish. Like dead dragons. Like dead dragons who had eaten rotten fish!" I pause, and Coco squints.

"What's the matter?" she says.

"I thought of a joke, but I don't know if you're old enough to hear it."

"Tell us."

"I don't think you're old enough."

"Tell us," they say. "Tell us, tell us!" They don't say the words, but I hear them anyway: *Our father is dead. For God's sake, tell us your joke.*

"Okay. A girl says to her boyfriend: 'Does my breath smell like tacos?' And she breathes on his face, like this." I exhale enthusiastically. "Her boyfriend draws back and says: 'I don't know. Do you put cat shit on your tacos?'"

Three separate looks of astonishment. No laughter.

"You're not supposed to use that word," Saltine Teacup says.

"You guys made me tell you the joke."

"That's a naughty word," says Pepper.

"I know," I say. "I'm sorry." And then I tell them how their mother and I used to scream and yell over the bad words when we listened to the eight-track of *Grease* while our father drove us to private school in Cambridge.

I tuck the folder of pictures back in my duffel bag and turn out the light. Through the sliding glass doors, we can see the leaves of the tulip tree shiver in the breeze.

"Let's go outside, to pray," Coco says.

"I think you're supposed to be trying to fall asleep now," I say. Their mother is asleep on a cot in the kitchen, and we'd have to walk through that room in order to get outside.

"Mommy won't mind," she says.

"Mommy will mind," I say, but before I can say anything else, she has tiptoed through the kitchen and is sliding open the glass door.

She gets down on her knees on the concrete and prays to her father. The sky above her is a flock of stars.

"I love you, Tata," she says. "You will always be the best daddy in the whole world. Always and forever and ever." I never saw a man more devoted to his kids. When he came home from work, at the sound of his voice, there would be a stampede for the door.

I kneel beside her and take her hands. "Your father loved you very much," I say.

"I know," Coco says.

Suddenly her mother is standing over us. "That's enough now," she says. "It's time for bed."

After Coco is asleep, I hover awkwardly in the kitchen. "Can I make you some hot chocolate, or anything?"

"No, thanks," my sister says. "I'm not really hungry. I just want to try to get back to sleep." And a moment later, she's in her cot on the other side of the room.

I don't want to admit that our grieving has not brought us closer together. If anything, it seems to have accentuated our differences. I believe in God; my sister does not. She lets me talk to her kids about God, and even wants them to take religious education classes, and receive their First Communion, but I know it's a strain for her. The strain has been added to of late. A couple cornered her at the funeral and said: "If you don't believe in Jesus, you'll never see your husband again." I was flabbergasted when she told me; all I could do was shake my head and apologize. I assume these people mean well, but I suspect statements like that only drive my sister farther away.

The next morning, we're back at the House of Pancakes. Same booth, same sweet waiter. After he takes our order, he tells me I have beautiful children. This is a misperception I not only allow, but encourage. I never correct the girls when they call me Mommy. They only do so when we're out in public—at home, they have a legit Mommy—and I get a secret thrill every time they do. When has motherhood ever come so cheap? None of the diapers, all of the fun. For years, I've kept a list of places I want to take them when they're older: the British Museum Reading Room; the garden at the Musée Rodin in Paris; Sant'Eustachio Il Caffè in Rome; the Main Hall at Union Station in Washington, D.C., where the original sculptures caused a stir, so now the sentries hold modesty shields in front of their private parts. I've even planned out things I want to say. At Luray Caverns, in Virginia, there's an organ that plays through the stalactites and sta-lagmites. I've imagined taking the girls there, pointing at the earthen instrument, and saying: "Do you know what that means? That means someone once looked at those piles of mud and heard music."

Driving home from the House of Pancakes, we listen to a CD of the songs that played during the video portion of their father's memorial. The girls don't know that's what it is; they think it's a CD I've made. "Just Breathe" by Eddie Vedder. "Live Forever" by Billy Joe Shaver. "Wildflowers" by Tom Petty. They know the words by now, and for a few verses, we all sing:

"*You belong among the wildflowers,*
*You belong in a boat out at sea.*
*Sail away, kill off the hours.*
*You belong somewhere you feel free.*"

When we walk in the door, the phone starts to ring. "Maybe that's Daddy, calling from heaven!" Coco says. I try to give my sister an expression that says *I never sug-gested there were phones in heaven,* but I don't know if it tracks. She looks as if someone has just torn out her heart and handed her a box of ashes, which is exactly what someone has done. Her purse is over her shoulder, and she lets the machine take the call.

"I have to meet with my lawyer," she says. "Can you watch the girls for a couple of hours?"

"Sure," I say, nodding. "Of course."

It's started to rain, so I plant the kids in front of the TV. First they watch a show called *The Wiggles*. Then they want to watch *The Sound of Music* for the one hundred and seventieth time. "'*Edelweiss*,'" I'll tell them someday, "was my parents' wedding song." While they sit in a row on the bed with their eyes glued to the screen, I lie on the floor and lean my head against my duffel bag. Before I do, I remove the folder of pictures. I begin to flip through them. Here is my sister wearing pink plastic sunglasses with lenses in the shape of hearts. There she is with her hair twisted in buns on the sides of her head like Princess Leia. Here she is holding a plate of cookies and carrots while I display a letter we've just written to Santa. Now she's cradling a Siamese kitten like a baby. A line from a Richard Powers story I read recently comes to me: "He's amazed that this fate has been lying in wait his entire life."

Saltine Teacup climbs off the bed and comes over to lie down beside me. She may be quiet, but she sees. She sees everything.

"Why are you crying?" she says. I open my eyes, and on the screen, two teenagers in a gazebo are about to kiss.

"It's a sad movie," I say.

. . .

My sister walks through the door, holding a stack of mail, rain and tears streaking her face. Sometimes she lets herself cry in front of the girls—she wants them to know it's all right to be sad—but it's clear this is not one of those times. Her keys thunk in a heap on the counter, and she turns in a circle. I can tell she wants to hide, or maybe throw up, but there's nowhere to go. I usher the girls into the bedroom and give them my makeup kit to play with.

"What's wrong?" I ask, and wonder if I have ever in my life asked a more idiotic question. She hands me the stack of mail. On top is a doctor's postcard, addressed in her husband's handwriting, a reminder for his yearly pilot physical. For a second, I'm vulnerable to the doorbell fantasy myself. Could he secretly be alive somewhere, and sending himself postcards? Could he show up at the front door any minute?

"I don't want this," she says quietly. Her eyes are filled with desolation and restraint and fear. "I don't want this life without him in it." She succumbs, and weeps silently, standing in the center of the kitchen, her body trembling. All around us, the windows stream with rain. I stare beyond her at the refrigerator, not knowing what to do. It seems impossible that this has happened. There's a magnet on the fridge that says: INSTANT HUMAN. JUST ADD COFFEE.

After she has cried for a bit, a subtle formality enters her body. She straightens and says: "While I was at the lawyer's dealing with the insurance, he suggested I redo my will." She wipes her eyes, tucks her hair behind her ears. The tip of her nose is red, and once more, she reminds me of a version of herself I recognize from thirty years ago. "I need to know if you'd be willing to take the girls if anything ever happened to me."

"Me?"

"Who else?" She sighs. "It's okay if you don't want to. You just have to say so."

My body is frozen in place: feet on the tile floor, hands pressed against the counter. "I don't know," I say. "I'd have to think about that."

My sister says nothing. I realize I'm inventing things, but the words I impute to her expression are: *Well—think.* The room we're standing in begins to feel very, very small. I reach for the keys. "Is it all right if I use the car?"

"Sure," she says. "The girls have ballet at five. Where are you going?"

"I was thinking of going to church." Coco's head pops out of the doorway. Her face is painted like a harlequin doll's.

"I want to come to church," she says. Going to church is one of our favorite things to do together. "Can I, Mommy?"

"You can't go looking like that," my sister says.

"Sure she can," I say. A priest once told me a story about a homeless man who wandered into a cathedral and was stopped as he made his way down the aisle. "You can't be in here without a shirt and shoes," said the monsignor. The homeless man looked up at the figure on the cross. "He doesn't have any," he said.

On our way into town, I play with various phrases in my head. They all contain the word *but.* "I love you, and I love my nieces more than anything, but . . ." But I'm not sure I can accept such an important responsibility. . . . But

I'm not sure I'm qualified for such a responsibility. . . . But I would be lying to you if I said I wanted to be a mother.

The church is nearly empty. Coco and I slide into a pew up front, near the banks of candles. She crosses herself twice before taking a seat, and I know it's because she gets confused at the end about whether it goes up-down-right-left or up-down-left-right, so she does both. I notice a glass case behind the altar and it reminds me there's something I need to tell my sister about her husband, but I have no idea how to do it.

I glance around and am stunned that I've never before registered how maternal all the imagery is. Everywhere you look, there's a mother holding a baby. At five o'clock, these pews will fill with a dozen or so parishioners, usually older people; there have been times when the girls and I were the only ones without white hair. But for now, it's just us, and a lone woman over by the shrine to the Sacred Heart. For a second, she reminds me of a solitary, parallel-universe version of myself, and I think: *Is that it, then? Is this the day I'll look back on as the one on which the path of my life changed?* I prop my hands against my forehead like a visor, and pray my favorite one-word prayer: *Help.*

Coco wants to light a candle for her father. She does, and then we light one for my father, and then we light one for those who have no one to pray for them. When the initial flare of the flames excites her, I briefly wonder if you're not supposed to teach six-year-olds to play with matches. Then we bless ourselves with holy water and step out into the rain.

Driving home, we stop at a convenience store. We

hurry through the doors, holding hands. "Mommy, may I please have a pack of rainbow-stripe gum?"

I let go of her hand. "Don't call me that," I say.

"But you love it when we call you Mommy."

"Just—don't call me that today."

The man behind the counter eyes us with concern, no doubt skimming his memory banks for missing-children posters. I buy a stack of celebrity and fashion magazines to distract my sister, and he rings me up.

"Could I have a pack of American Spirits?" I say at the end. I can't believe these words are coming out of my mouth. I haven't smoked a cigarette in twelve years. "The yellow ones," I say.

In the car, I crack the windows and turn the air-conditioning on high. We idle in the parking lot while nicotine hits all the dormant receptors in my brain.

"Don't tell," I say, exhaling. "And don't ever smoke. It's really bad for you."

Coco starts to cough, and I think: *Right. This right here is why you have to say no.*

"Can we listen to the music?" she says. She pushes the power button, and Bob Dylan starts to sing a melancholy song about heaven.

"What's it like, where Daddy is?" she says.

"I don't know, honey. Please—don't ask me questions like that." The only thing that comes to mind is a clever advertisement I saw recently: *Beyond your wildest imagination. Exactly what you'd think.* "All I can tell you is I'm betting it's not all harps and clouds." The irony is that there have been days, other days, when I've sat in a car filled with music I loved with bright sun all around and a feeling of light flooding my veins, and thought: *This is the closest I'll come to heaven on Earth*. Now I'm sitting in the rain in a car I know has all my sister's husband's suits, belts, and shoes in the trunk. "I couldn't decide which would be less painful," she confessed. "To keep them, or to give them away."

I lean my forehead against the steering wheel, and Coco rubs my back. She doesn't ask what's the matter; she must be getting accustomed to adults behaving oddly.

"You have to follow your own path in life," I say. "Even if it feels guilty or selfish or wrong. It's the only way to live."

When we get home, Saltine Teacup runs to greet me. She wraps her arms around my waist and hides her face in my belly. I place my hand against her head, which is exactly where it would be if I were pregnant.

"Why didn't you take me with you?" she says. "I wanted to come to church, too."

My sister and I lock eyes above her, and the words just come out. "I'll do it," I say.


After dinner, after the girls are asleep, I hear my sister in the old empty house, keening. I have ears for her voice, and in spite of the distance, the night air soars with pain. It is a sound both fresh and ancient; my sister has joined a lineage of women she never wished to be a part of. *Someday*, I think, *I'll tell her*. Then I realize that someday is today.

She's lying on the floor of the master bedroom, in the

dark. She must have heard me enter the house, because she's stopped crying. I halt in the doorway.

"Can I come in?"

"Sure," she whispers. I walk over and lie down beside her. From the ceiling, electrical cords and metal tubes coil out of the Sheetrock like snakes.

"There's something I wanted to tell you," I say. With no furniture in the room, my voice makes an unexpected echo. "I did something, in the hospital, at the end." I hesitate. "I probably should have asked your permission first." My sister doesn't say anything, so I keep talking. I tell her how on one of the days in between when the stroke damaged his brain stem and the day he died, I anointed her husband. I gave him unction. I have some holy oil that was blessed by the bishop who performed my Confirmation, and I brought it with me on the plane, in a plastic container that used to hold Neutrogena lip gloss. I describe how I dipped my fingers in the oil, and laid them on her husband's wrists, and on his feet, and on his side. I tell her how I made the sign of the cross on his forehead, and blessed him. And how, at the end, I held my hand for a long time over his heart, his beautiful heart. I don't tell her how unworthy I felt to the task, or how I remembered some lines of Annie Dillard's, and uttered them before I began: "Who shall ascend the hill of the Lord? Or who shall stand in his holy place? There is no one but us. . . . There never has been."

When I've finished, we both lie still in the silence. I can hear my pulse in my ears. My sister turns to me.

"You had no right to do that," she says.

"I know. I guess I figured it wouldn't do any harm."

"You figured it wouldn't do any harm? That's why you did it?"

My eyes have adjusted, and I can see now that the room is filled with pale moonlight. "I loved him, too, you know," I say.

"You loved him from a distance," my sister says. "Your favorite way to love."

"Excuse me?"

"In my world, we don't show people we love them by pouring oil on them when they die. We show people we love them by spending time with them when they're alive."

I don't have an answer to that, so I stand up.

"Why don't you leave," my sister says.

"I'm leaving."

"No, I mean—why don't you go home."

The next morning, when I wake up, I find a napkin on top of the folder of pictures.

*I'm sorry,* my sister has written. *Please stay.* I pick it up and carry it with me into the kitchen, where she's sitting at the computer.

"*You're* sorry," I say. "What are *you* sorry for? *I'm* sorry!"

"Thank you for being here," she says. "I appreciate it." I put my hand on her shoulder, and this time, she lets it remain.

She stands up. "Where'd you get those pictures?"

"I stole them from Mom."

"Would you mind if I scanned them into the computer?"

"Not at all," I say. She gets the folder and begins to scan them, one by one, while I sit with her. There's a framed wedding photograph on her desk of her with her arms around her husband under a canopy of leaves; they are nose to nose. She unscrews the back and removes the photo. Then she places it facedown and leaves her palm against it while the light rolls by. Everything around us reeks of life: the blooming tulip trees, the fresh coffee brewing, the sun-dappled pool. I hear voices, and a moment later, the kids are spilling into the room. Coco opens the refrigerator. Pepper clambers into my lap. Saltine Teacup's eyes are even bluer when she first wakes up. She takes one of the photos from her mother's stack.

"What's this?" she says.

"That's the house we lived in when you were first born," my sister says.

"It is?" she says. She doesn't remember anything from that time; she was too young. My sister's husband, aware of how sick he was, had said at the end: "But if I die now, the girls won't remember me."

"That's the house where they wanted to make your daddy cut his hedge, but then he went around and took pictures of the hedges of all the city council members, and they stopped," I say.

My sister smiles. I haven't seen her smile in so long.

"We will always tell you stories about your father," I say to the girls. "You won't ever forget him." When they're old enough, I will tell them how when he died, their mother had said: "You were the best thing that ever happened to me," and had climbed into the hospital bed and lain down beside him. One day I will tell them how I watched her weep at the memorial while gigantic pictures flashed on a screen above our heads, and the whole auditorium swelled with the music of their wedding song: "I Just Want to Dance with You." Someday I will tell them about the hiking trip where he spontaneously stripped off all his clothes and jumped into the Merced River. One day I'll tell them how I once saw him change a diaper with one hand, after he'd broken his wrist, and I thought: *Now I've seen everything.* Someday I will let them read this story.

## Author's Notes

I love it when authors share the backstories to stories and snippets about their creative process. So I thought I would part the veil and share my own.

### THAT OF WHICH WE CANNOT SPEAK

In my twenties, for about a year and a half, I smoked. I was never very good at it, but the real catalyst for quitting was an extremely educational two-week bout of laryngitis. Somewhere in my files there's a photograph of me from a party I attended during this humbling, voiceless fortnight. It's taken from behind, and at first looks like a throwaway shot. Only on closer inspection can you see the piece of package string tied at the back of my neck.

Although I'm more physically allied with Samantha, it was Bradley's emotional struggle that resonated with me. Giving voice to the inner life and speaking the truth even when I know it won't be well-received are ongoing battles. There's an art to being both honest and gentle, and a sadness to always erring on the side of caution, as Bradley does. I'm personally so fascinated by people who are not restrained by a fear of disapproval that I once stared in awe at a man who was clipping his fingernails in the lobby of the midtown office building where I worked. Although it's true that when I related this story to a friend, she said: "Well, let's not confuse lack of self-consciousness with schizophrenia."

While working on this story, I was haunted by a quote by Thomas de Quincey: "If in this world there is one misery having no relief, it is the pressure on the heart from the Incommunicable." I kept wondering if the pressure was pure misery, or if there might not be some pleasure in it.

### THE ONLY WAY OUT IS THROUGH

Lee K. Abbott once told me that a good story should cost the writer more than just time and ink. There were a couple of moments while I was working on "Through" that I had to stop typing, put my head down, and let myself cry. I straightened up after one such break, remembered Lee's advice, and thought: *Well, maybe this one will be good.*

In typical fashion, I accumulated piles of research about camping—including purchasing and reading the book referred to (they really *were* out of *Camping for Dummies*)—only to write a story in which the characters never actually camp. Which I can't hold against them.

I don't mind being outdoors occasionally; I just don't feel the need to sleep there. I had numerous alternate silly names for Fetterman's band—naming being one of the best reasons to form a band—including 60 PhDs, Command Z, and Undisclosed Location.

Martin Lee Anderson is the name of a real teen boot-camp casualty. Once I'd been moved by his experience, I didn't want to change his name, so I gave him a cameo. It was only after I'd written this story that I saw the parallel between the way it ends and the Bible's Abraham and Isaac.

## GOOD IN A CRISIS

Some years ago I ran a personal ad that began: "Blond, blue-eyed Harvard grad, 29, seeks kind and brilliant man who is intellectually uninhibited, socially independent, and spiritually intrigued." It was an unmitigated disaster. Most of the respondents who didn't sound as if they kept their mother's body in a bag in the basement said such things as: "I'm not at all what you're looking for, but I liked your ad." Although it didn't lead to romance, I guess you could say the hours spent reading the ads of others helped spawn this story. And the experience of writing an ad was invaluable, if for no other reason than the challenge of trying to reconcile, in words, a love of solitude with the desire for companionship. I came across a single poet in LA who did it fairly well: "Particularly interested in those who do not squirm in quietude."

My public high school in Winchester, Massachusetts,

was (and still is) such an arcadia of gifted teachers that
I often wish I'd had the sense to capitalize on my good
fortune at the time. Just one more example of *too soon
old, too late smart*. The year I wrote this story was the
same year I finally got around to writing a thank-you
note to one of my favorite teachers—Fran Russell, head
of the English department—only to hear back, in a
lovely handwritten letter from her sister, that she'd died
a few months earlier.

There was another teacher, a charismatic and
attractive English teacher I had sophomore year, who
later disappeared. I suppose "Crisis" was partly the
result of my wondering what had happened to him.

For a long time while I was working on this story,
an odious invention known as grammar check kept
suggesting I rewrite the second sentence as: "The
language people mesmerized her." This was highly
annoying until I realized that, indeed, the language
people do.


THE THING ITSELF

I've always enjoyed the fiction in *The Atlantic Monthly*,
and at one point someone told me that they really like
stories where something happens. Which I do, too; I love
humor, and insight, and language, but I think most of
all, I love stories where something of genuine importance
to the characters is at stake, and I don't think it's a crime
for literary fiction to be suspenseful or entertaining. So
after I heard this, I went home and wrote the opening

lines: "Something was about to happen. He could feel it." And immediately I thought: *Aha! Now I've got it!*

In the truly gloomy days that followed, it slowly dawned on me that now that I'd set the stakes, I was going to have to find a way to live up to them. Which of course wound up being a tremendous gift, and in the process of trying to do so, I was able to allow the story to surprise even me.

*Nota Bene:* This story has an ending that not all readers grasp the first time through. So I will offer this hint: Janet has news of her own.

Special thanks to ZZ Packer, for choosing "The Thing Itself" to win the 2008 Arts & Letters Prize.

## THE LAZIEST FORM OF REVELATION

A writer friend and I had just decided that the best way to write dialogue that didn't feel overly crafted was to put in everything you want, then go back and take out half of it. No sooner did we come up with this rule than I began to exploit its opposite, and found myself working on a story about a woman who couldn't stop talking. The more her painter-boyfriend ignored her (even as he studied her), the more she felt compelled to reveal.

I have some strawberry in my hair, and part of me has always wished I were a true redhead. In the middle of working on this story, I had lunch with my great-aunt, Corinne Black, whose college nickname was "Torchy." It was she who told me her mother would never allow her to sit as close to the fire as other family members because she was afraid Corinne's head would ignite. As soon as I heard the anecdote, I knew I wanted to use it (that's what the pocket tape recorder I always keep with me is for). I sure hope I was the one who bought the chicken-salad sandwiches that day.

## THE SUMMER BEFORE

"The Summer Before" was the first short story I ever wrote—not counting grade school compositions, including one about the adventures a baseball has after it's hit out of the park. It languished in a drawer for fifteen years—my coming-of-age story, waiting to come of age. I think because the characters are so young, this story in particular brings to mind Irving Howe's wonderful observation: "The best art almost becomes sentimental, but doesn't." During one of my editing sessions, I cut a line in which a yacht passes by with the words *Writer's Block* emblazoned across its stern. It didn't fit with the rest of the scene, and once I realized how bizarrely attached to it I was, I knew it had to go. Lifted from real life was the yellow outboard christened *Lightning Bug,* which belonged to Bruce and Mark Ashmun, who were part of a gang of friends who helped make summers at Lake Winnipesaukee the kind of thing you want to grow up and write about.

I'm the oldest of four girls, and if I were ever forced to watch a movie of my life—for the purpose of instruction, if not judgment—I'm certain there would be numerous scenes during which I would have to look away, for shame. I suppose this story was one way of trying to do penance. It is dedicated to my sisters.

Lastly: Before he met my mother, my father was engaged to a woman named Fran (Frances Marshall Watkins), who died of Lou Gehrig's disease. I'm glad she gets to play a small role in this story, unlike the rather large role she plays in my life: Had she not died, I would never have lived.

## MOLLUSK MAKES A COMEBACK

Some stories are born whole; they arrive almost seamlessly, and all you can do is humbly acknowledge them as the gifts they are. This was not one of those stories. "Mollusk" lived on my computer for twelve years before it was published, and had different titles and varying details. But its heart remained the same. To me, it's a story about a young woman's search for something to believe in, and her attempts to muster the conviction to live.

Katie has become a bit of a cult figure for my sisters and me. We still speak of "pulling a Katie" or "having a total Katie Day." Although we like to imply it's all other people's fault, usually it means coming face-to-face with the impossibility of staying on top of everything. A Katie Day is a day where everything goes wrong at once, typically in a sad, slightly funny way—the only upside to chaos being that it frequently spits out a joke.

I tend to be drawn to people like Katie, who lived through some period of aimlessness or recklessness before they found their feet. It seems I'm able to spot them across a crowded room. Or if I don't spot them, they spot me. Even though Katie is a mess in a lot of ways, she also has a lot to teach.

## I KNEW YOU'D BE LOVELY

I wrote this story while I was at the Iowa Writers' Workshop for a summer. I'd taken up smoking while I was there—it seemed the thing to do—and my old Mac desktop conked out mid-story, possibly from nicotine exposure. (The only Mac to ever fail me, and I don't blame the embattled machine one bit.) I had no car at the time, and I remember waiting with excruciating impatience for a bus to come and take me to the campus writing lab before I forgot everything. Once back at one of their computers, I feverishly tried to reconstruct what I'd written, which was utterly strange: I'm not used to working on stories with other people around, during normal business hours.

"Lovely" became my first published story when Joan Silber chose it to win the *Inkwell* Writing Competition in 2007. I will always be indebted to her and to the other lovelies at *Inkwell*.

## PROOF OF LOVE

I wrestled with this story while writing it, keenly aware of the fine line between a *character* who has strong opinions and a *story* that has strong opinions, and the cosmic No-No of finding yourself on the wrong side of that line. (Samuel Goldwyn: "If you have a message, send a telegram.") I knew Kelly's persona intimately, so she was easy to write; and I hadn't seen her elsewhere, so I wanted to write her. But insecurity about the story endured. For that reason, I've been especially surprised at the warm reception it has received—one admirer made a PROOF OF LOVE T-shirt; another defended my own character to me: "She's not a Jesus freak! She's freaky for Jesus!" I love these people, and don't think my gratitude can be fully expressed.

## WE'VE GOT A GREAT FUTURE BEHIND US

When I left New York City, I chose Pawling, New York, partly because of a wonderful live-music venue they have here called the Towne Crier Café. A few winters ago, I heard Jon Poussette-Dart perform there. He introduced one of his songs by saying it was the result of a collaboration between him and two friends; they'd promised when they were married that they'd write a song with him, and had honored the promise even after they acrimoniously divorced. I loved the idea so much, I don't think I slept that night. His song was not called "We've Got a Great Future Behind Us"—in fact, I don't recall it being self-referential at all—but nonetheless, a story was born.

I originally thought "Future" was going to be about an estranged couple airing their grievances with each other while writing love songs—*through* the lyrics of the songs—which just shows you what too much caffeine can do.

Around the time I wrote this, I dated a man who left

me speechless when he said he thought women shouldn't be allowed to vote because we let our feelings distort our perceptions. It was a shocking statement from an otherwise decent man, and I can remember wondering whether I should tell him: "When you date the woman who comes after me, you might want to leave that little nugget in your purse."

DOUBLE-BLIND

The inspiration for this story came from a passage in a book Perry Mehrling wrote about my father, Fischer Black. In the fall of 1961, my dad shared a small apartment at 1560 Cambridge Street with three physicists and an historian. For some reason, the idea of sharing a kitchen and a bathroom with three physicists fascinated me. Perry's book also taught me that in high school, my dad and some of his friends had formed a group called the American Society of Creators, Apostles and Prophets—possibly named for the American Society of Composers, Authors and Publishers—whose stated purpose was "to try to work out effective methods of true discussion." These two things combined to create the initial spark for "Double-Blind." As is often the case, many of the original details never made it to the final draft, e.g., that the group read *Scientific American* and would then discuss Norbert Wiener's cybernetic theory of the human nervous system, or how Aldous Huxley's ideas on altered states of consciousness led them to try their hands at hypnosis.

Of course, the well-known line about bumblebees

not being able to fly according to the laws of physics is a famous mischaracterization; what bumblebees can't theoretically do is *coast*.

THE FAR SIDE OF THE MOON

This story was first conceived as an entry for an *Esquire* fiction contest, in which I was trying to write a story to go with the title "Twenty-Ten." I didn't win, but I'm nonetheless grateful to them; if it weren't for their contest, I never would have written the story.

People sometimes ask if it's difficult to write in the male voice, and for whatever reason, I don't find it to be. "Moon" was one of my easiest stories to write; I think it took me only about three weeks (the contest deadline helped). I laughed appreciatively when a male reader told me it was a quintessential male-voice story, saying: "It could be subtitled 'Sex, drugs, rock and roll, and cars. And beer.'"

My uncle Carl tamed the squirrels when he was a freshman at Harvard and would then impress women with his authority over small woodland creatures. He also had a roommate on whom the character of Ace is loosely based. Ace was a writer's dream—what's more fun than a character who says yes to everything?—and in many ways, his spirit lives on in a new book I'm working on, *The Lucky Brother*.

# Acknowledgments

Heartfelt thanks to: Lee K. Abbott, Carl Allen, Miriam Allen, Ted Allen, Matthew Arkin, Lisa Bankoff, Blakeney Bartlett, Anne Bartoc, Anna Becker, Beverly Bell, Vilem Benes, Ashley Black, Christina Black, Fischer Black, Kerry Black, Lee and CeCe Black, Melissa Black, Mimi Black, Paige Black, all my friends at *Bloomberg Business Week,* Beth Boswell, Dennis Boutsikaris, Guy Boyd, Alexa Brandenberg, Aaron Brown, Suzanne Brownstein, Robert Byrnes, Bill Camp, Stephen Cavitt, Clay McLeod Chapman, Julia Coffey, Margo Crespin, Alice Elliott Dark, Aleta Davies, Sarah Davis, Alex Dawson, Danielle DeVine, Rebecca Donner, Peter Eicher, Marc Fitten, Cynthia Flaxenburg, Robert Fogarty, Elliott Forrest, Brian Frazer, David Gates, Anney Giobbe, Nicole Goguen, Natalie Goldberg, Peter Hayes, Randell Haynes, Joshua Henkin, George Herrmann, Robin Hirsch, Ron Hogan, Hillary Holloway, Emily Barton Hopkins, Tom Jenks, Thom Jones, Joy Katz, Jennie Kaufman, Céline Keating, John

Kennedy, the Kiley sisters, Autumn Kindelspire, Valerie Leff, Alex Lindquist, David Lynn, Steve McCarthy, Perry Mehrling, N. Scott Momaday, Christianna Nelson, Jim O'Grady, Larry O'Keefe, Anne O'Sullivan, ZZ Packer, David Palecek, David Pengilly, Paul Plissey, Sharon Pomerantz, Spence Porter, Chris Power, Christine Pride, Patricia Randell, M. Z. ("Reb Zed") Ribalow, Joshua Roberts, David Rocks, Rick Rofihe, Diane Salvatore, Scott Sanderson, Alex Sapountzis, Jonathan Schorr, Campbell Scott, John Shea, Ian Sheehy, Isaiah Sheffer, Joan Silber, Bill Silverman, Linda Simone, Gerry Skinder, Robbyn Spratt, Scott Stossel, Jill Sverdlove, Jim Taibi, the Tawes family, Michelle Toth, Grant Tracey, Brenda Ueland, Michael Voll, Eric Vrooman, Craig Wall, David Wallace-Wells, Susan Walter, Alexis Washam, Rob Weatherbee, Matthew Wells, Bob Whelan, Ron Witmer, Yeshua, Sarah Young, Steve Zimmer, and a standing ovation to Jeff Jackson.

The author wishes to thank the editors of the following publications, in which these stories first appeared: "That of Which We Cannot Speak" in *The Antioch Review,* "The Only Way Out Is Through" in *Narrative,* "Good in a Crisis" in *The North American Review,* "The Thing Itself" in *Arts & Letters* (winner of the 2008 Prize for Fiction), "The Laziest Form of Revelation" in *The Kenyon Review,* "Mollusk Makes a Comeback" in *The Chattahoochee Review,* "I Knew You'd Be Lovely" in *Inkwell* (winner of the 2007 Fiction Competition), "Proof of Love" in *American Literary Review,* "We've Got a Great Future Behind Us" in *Green Mountains Review,* and "Double-Blind" in *The Saint Ann's Review.*